THE

Edgardo Cozari⸺ ⸺⸺ ⸺s Aires
in 1939 and now ⸺⸺⸺me between that
city and Paris. Bes⸺nown for his subtle, semi-
documentary films, he is the author of two
notable short-story collections, *The Bride from
Odessa* and *Urban Voodoo*.

Nick Caistor's translations from the Spanish and
Portuguese include works by Juan Marsé, Eduardo
Mendoza, Sergio Ramírez, José Saramago, Carlos
María Domínguez and Osvaldo Soriano.

ALSO BY EDGARDO COZARINSKY

The Bridge from Odessa

EDGARDO COZARINSKY

The Moldavian Pimp

TRANSLATED FROM THE SPANISH BY
Nick Caistor

WITH AN AFTERWORD BY
Alberto Manguel

VINTAGE BOOKS
London

Published by Vintage 2007

2 4 6 8 10 9 7 5 3 1

Copyright © Edgardo Cozarinsky and Emecé Editores S.A. 2004
English translation copyright © Nick Caistor 2006
Afterword copyright © Alberto Manguel 2005

Edgardo Cozarinsky has asserted his right under the Copyright,
Designs and Patents Act 1988 to be identified as the author
of this work

First published with the title *El rufián moldavo*
By Emecé Editores S.A. in 2004

First published in Great Britain in 2006 by
Harvill Secker
Random House, 20 Vauxhall Bridge Road,
London SW1V 2SA

www.vintage-books.co.uk

Addresses for companies within The Random House Group Limited
can be found at: www.randomhouse.co.uk/offices.htm

The Random House Group Limited Reg. No. 954009

A CIP catalogue record for this book
is available from the British Library

ISBN 9780099483755

Mixed Sources
Product group from well-managed
forests and other controlled sources
www.fsc.org Cert no. TT-COC-2139
© 1996 Forest Stewardship Council

FSC

Printed in the UK by CPI Bookmarque, Croydon, CR0 4TD

To talk of the living I need
words the dead have taught me

ALBERTO TABBIA

PART ONE

I

"STORIES AREN'T MADE UP, THEY'RE INHERITED."

The old man's voice was soft but steady.

"It's dangerous to make up stories. If they're any good, they end up coming true. After a while they get passed on, and by then it's no longer important that they were made up: there'll always be someone who has lived them."

He coughed, and after a pause added:

"Anyway, I couldn't give a damn about stories."

The nurse came over with some blankets. Despite her professional smile, there was no disguising the ice in her voice:

"Grandad here isn't used to visitors. They'll be serving supper in a minute, and if he doesn't have a rest he'll get stomach-ache."

She was staring straight at me. I had no option but to stand up. On my way out, I dropped a hand onto the old man's shoulder and whispered:

"I'll come back to see you next Sunday."

But three days later he died, and I was left with so many unanswered questions.

* * *

I think it was the first time I visited that I heard him say something about dreams being the only means the dead have to communicate with us.

I can still hear his voice: "Has it never struck you that in dreams we don't see dead people in their graves, or in the coffins we saw them in for the last time when we were standing vigil over them? They're at our side, walking, eating, arguing, fighting with us. I sometimes wonder if God didn't give us the capacity to dream just so that the dead can communicate with us, or so that we can see a bit more of those who have departed."

"Where did you read that? It doesn't sound like the Talmud to me . . ."

"My teacher used to tell me that. He was from Vilnius."

Naming the Lithuanian capital brought tears brimming to his eyes. I had never seen him like that before, and was afraid he might burst out crying. I said quickly:

"Come on, get your coat and I'll take you for a drink in the bar on the corner."

"I think it closed down last week."

"It was open half an hour ago when I went past."

He opened his wardrobe and I caught a glimpse of two pairs of trousers and a synthetic wool jacket with a white furry lining. "Poor man, his daughter-in-law must have given it him," I thought, but then remembered that his son lived in Paris and his daughter-in-law had settled in Barcelona.

The pavement was like an obstacle course of holes. It had been raining since morning, and what was left of the concrete was treacherous. With an affectionate gesture, I put a hand on his shoulder to disguise my fear he might slip.

The bar was open, but empty. Generations of unwary flies had accumulated on the neon strips, which had apparently not been cleaned since the 1950s, and shed a feeble aquarium-light on the modest decor. Behind the bar were mirrors that created a double image of the bottles lined up on glass shelves, but seemed long ago to have given up on the task of offering a clear image of anyone standing in front of them. Among the bottles I could spot labels I had not seen for years: Legui and Mariposa rums, Amargo Obrero bitters, La Bella Friulana grappa.

"Marble table-tops . . . in any other neighbourhood they would be a luxury," I said. "You can't even find wooden ones these days, formica is everywhere."

The old man glanced suspiciously at the tables; he seemed put out. He surveyed me in silence before speaking:

"I spend the whole day sitting down or in bed. I prefer to stand up at the bar for a while."

So we stood there, facing our blurred images in the mirror, drinking some unknown make of grappa: the La

5

Bella Friulana bottle was empty, the bar owner explained. He kept it for decoration, as a memento; he couldn't remember how long it had been since the distillery closed down. He chatted to the old man about some bits of neighbourhood gossip: the next-door garage that would soon be moving, the lot opposite that was still empty because of an inheritance dispute. I realised the two men knew each other.

"I can't imagine you living in this neighbourhood. I can't see you far from Calle Corrientes in the centre. How long have you been in the Home?"

"Centuries. I can't travel very far, because I get tired. And anyway, this bar is no worse than any other in Villa Crespo."

He paused, then said to the owner:

"Shame it's going to shut, isn't it?"

The owner acknowledged this with a doubtful grunt, then launched into a confused explanation, the gist of which I took to be that he couldn't find a buyer, not because he was asking too much, but because they all wanted to pay in instalments, and he didn't like the idea.

"They think that because they're talking dollars I'm bound to accept," he explained. "But if I do, all I'll see is the down payment. That's why I prefer to stay until I'm carried out feet first."

The bar owner had only walked a couple of steps away from us when the old man spoke in what he thought was a whisper intended just for me:

"He'll never leave. Too many memories. He's not like the people who run the garage. This neighbourhood is dying, and he'll go with it."

The afternoon light was fading rapidly on that cold August winter day. When the old man refused a second glass of grappa, I walked him back to the Home before night fell. A dubious nurse was waiting for us in the hall. ("Did you wrap up properly, Don Samuel? This damp is worse than the cold, you know.") I said goodbye until the following Sunday.

"In the end I didn't get to show you my collection of theatre programmes. We talked about everything else, except what really interests you."

"We'll look at them together next Sunday, and you can tell me all about them."

* * *

I only finally got to see the programmes several weeks later. They were in a shoe-box on the top shelf of the wardrobe. "Take whatever you like as a souvenir," the director of the Home had suggested, after explaining to me, half-accusing, half-apologising, that I had never left them my phone number, and that when the old man "took a turn for the worse" on the previous Wednesday, they had hardly had time to call an ambulance, and that he had died before reaching the Israelita Hospital. He had been buried on Friday in La Tablada cemetery. Could I possibly inform his son? They didn't have his details; all they knew was that he lived in Paris. I didn't know where either, but I could try to find out.

Empty, the room looked narrower than when the old man dragged his feet tirelessly across it, grumbling because he could not find his newspaper, or to pull a packet of the cigarettes he was forbidden to smoke out of the cushion cover. The transistor radio had already disappeared. On the tiny bedside table next to the heater I saw the pack of dried figs I had brought him a few weeks earlier. It was almost empty, as was the bag of *kasha* in the wardrobe that I had left for him. Was that all he had eaten?

"His clothes and shoes might come in useful for someone in the Home," I told the director as I said goodbye. I showed him the shoe-box full of papers. "I'll take these theatre programmes as something to remember him by. After I've been through them, I'll donate them to a library."

He had nothing against my suggestion; in fact, he seemed pleased I was leaving the few bits of clothes, which might be of some value to him. I suspect his smile was somewhat condescending towards an idiot who was obsessed by old scraps of paper announcing performances no longer being put on, in theatres that no longer existed, with actors who had been dead for decades. I didn't bother to explain that it was precisely because they were phantoms, shreds of a lost world, that they were important to me. While the bus took me along almost deserted streets and blind housefronts, as if nobody even wanted to look out on such

8

a miserable and rainy Sunday afternoon, through the window I watched the feeble light of day fade as we made our way to the centre of Buenos Aires. I kept a tight hold of the box on my lap, as though I was afraid I might lose it. All at once I could not wait until we reached Colegiales, and so I opened it.

The programmes were not leaflets, but small posters. Long and narrow, at the top they had the name of the theatre – the Soleil, the Excelsior, or the Ombú – occasionally a photograph of the famous star on tour (such as Jacob Ben Ami or Molly Picon), then their name and the title of the play in big Hebrew and Latin characters. In smaller letters, but still in both languages, were two columns with the details of the cast, the days and times of performances, the price of tickets. There were all sorts of different quality papers: some were still pristine and had a satin sheen to them; others were very thin and had blue and red inks printed cheaply on them in an attempt to make the presentation more attractive.

I wouldn't say that the interminable bus journey flew by, but as we rumbled through less poverty-stricken neighbourhoods, or ones less resigned to their poverty, and neon lights from pizzerias, video-clubs and supermarkets began to punctuate the darkness, it gradually occurred to me that some of these handbills must be for shows the old man or his wife had been in. And in fact I soon discovered the names Sami Warschauer and Perla Ritz, although it took an effort to associate the man in the photograph (thin quiff of hair, top lip emphasised by the line of a pencil moustache, and a halo of light behind his head as was the fashion with professional photography of those days) with the old man I had visited on three or four Sundays in the Doctor Mauricio Frenkel Home. It was the librarian at the Institute who had put me on to him: "So you're interested in Yiddish theatre? There are not many of those people left. Old man Warschauer was still alive in an old people's home in Avellaneda not so long ago. He used to be in musical revues at the Soleil." Beneath the peroxide-blonde hair and the eyebrows plucked to form two perfect arcs, I discovered that Perla Ritz had features typical of any actress of undefinable age who might be featured between the covers of *Antena* or *Radiolandia* magazines.

The theatre progamme I found with their names was from May 1945. As was obligatory at that time, it celebrated the defeat of Nazism. Sami and Perla smiled from photographs which quite possibly had been taken ten years earlier, in a less optimistic era. The show was called *Victory Revue*. I stroked the piece of paper, as though to touch something which had survived (even if only in a pile of old papers, in a shoe-box, at the back of a wardrobe, in a suburban old people's home) all the disappointments that followed that victory.

All at once I realised I had gone past my stop.

2

A FEW DAYS LATER I HELD IN MY HANDS A FADED CARD-board folder containing 120 pages of typescript on that very thin paper known in the days of typewriters as "onionskin". The title of the work was written on the cover in blue ink in Hebrew characters, and in the same colour ink someone unused to the Latin alphabet had carefully traced the translation: "Victory Revue".

This encounter took place in less than picturesque surroundings: the reading-room of the Theatre History Institute, in the basement of the Cervantes Theatre. I let myself be led by a vague assistant, whose memory seemed more reliable than the grubby handwritten card indexes she lived among. Thanks to her, in the depths of the archive I discovered some dusty rather than gloomy shelves devoted to the seasons of Yiddish theatre whose existence I had stumbled across a few months earlier. They were phantoms from a distant past, and all at once this underground library seemed to me a cave full of promise and mystery. Curious, not in the least apprehensive, I let the ghosts come towards me.

"How is it that a young man like you, who's not even Jewish, is interested in this sort of thing . . . the Yiddish theatre died out, and now not even the Jews are interested in what used to be": my supervisor in the School of Journalism was keen for me to find a less out-of-the way topic for my dissertation. I didn't know what to say. I wasn't going to start explaining to him that despite my impeccably Italian surname, my mother was called Finkelstein: that would have been to give in to the kind of determinism I cannot accept. If I told him that everything to do with what was fashionable and the latest trends depressed me, he would think I was a precocious snob. Nor could I tell him that it was the archaeology of the recent past which really fascinated me: I'm not a university professor, and terms like that are reserved for academe. As on other occasions in my life, which people persist in regarding as short even though I feel I have lived through and can remember much more than my twenty-five years might suggest, I preferred to pay no attention to his objections, however well meant. I do not like admitting to those who might poke fun at my naïvety that deep down I see myself as a detective, a private eye who, since reality does not provide me with any dangerous investigations, has to seek them out among other people's papers and remembrances.

The folder I had in front of me offered me one such adventure. When I opened it, I soon realised that the contents were different from the title on the cover. The first page, also written in both alphabets, announced: "The Moldavian Pimp".

* * *

What did the theatre mean to people who had lived before me? Until well into the twentieth century, painted backdrops and a few frequently restyled and dyed costumes, with the help of coloured lights from an age when the invention of dimmers and non-manual devices was still unheard of, could plunge the avid spectator of theatrical illusion into the realms of glorious lost empires or the mysteries of dreams. As with reading, characters and adventures come to life in our imagination, like those Japanese paper flowers which when submerged in a glass of water unfold, revealing unsuspected petals and colours.

I know these are well-worn metaphors, but I use them simply to suggest the excitement with which one winter afternoon in Buenos Aires I gradually left behind that reading-room, with its workaday furniture and strictly functional lighting, to float for two hours in a world of brightly coloured silhouettes, as changing as the fleeting shapes seen through a kaleidoscope, and to be stirred by real passion. That is how I came to lose myself in a play entitled *The Moldavian Pimp*, attracted less by the surprise of coming across something different from what I had expected from the cover than by the title's cheap seduction.

I was relieved to find the play was written in Spanish.

Some expressions in brackets penned in Yiddish, especially the titles of the musical numbers, led me to think there must be another version of the text, probably the original, which had been the one actually staged. Perhaps this translation was for some city authority that had to approve the play, although I'm not sure whether censorship officially existed at the time (what time?) when the work was first put on. But had it in fact ever been performed? Later on the Institute's helpful files were to inform me that after four performances at the Ombú Theatre in the street of the same name (nowadays Calle Pasteur), *The Moldavian Pimp* had been in repertory for two whole seasons (1927 and 1928) in two of the lesser-known theatres on Calle Corrientes.

The curtain rises on a joyful scene on the banks of the River Prut in Kishinev. ("A painted backdrop suggests a river-bank sloping down to the river; in the distance we can see the far bank, woods, and a sunset.") A group of young girls is laughing and dancing together; some older women are laying trays of the inevitable poppyseed and cheesecakes on trestle tables. It seems to be a birthday celebration. The suggested accompanying music is a *freilach*, which is interrupted by the arrival of "a good-looking young man, tall, with black hair and sad eyes". He is carrying a violin, but it is not he who plays the violin solo which takes over from the orchestra as he sings "Farewell my friends, I'm leaving for America . . ." The mournful strains of the song bring tears to the young girls' eyes. As he reaches the last verse ("If I only had a wife to travel with me . . .") his tearful audience suddenly becomes all of a flutter. The girls rush round the heartbroken singer and sing in chorus: "Take me with you, I want to see America . . ." The older women make useless attempts to hold them back, sighing with despair as they do so. "Like the Pied Piper of Hamelin", the leading man circles the stage before leaving it, closely followed by his retinue of singing admirers.

Even before the curtain rises, the second scene is announced by a solo on the bandoneon. (The script suggests either "Derecho Viejo", or "El Marne".) This time we are onboard a ship at dawn; effects called for — sea breeze and the cries of gulls. One by one, the girls troop on stage, and stare out at the seascape ("the ship's rail corresponds to the edge of the stage; the actors peer at the horizon as if it were in the back row of the stalls") until one of them shouts: "Where's the statue of Liberty?" A musical number expresses their anxiety: a syncopated rhythm and overlapping refrains ("Where are we? What's the port we can see in the distance?"). At this point, the troubled young man from the first scene makes his reappearance. Now he is smiling and enthusiastic, and is carrying a bandoneon instead of a violin. He sings in splendid baritone: "We are going to discover a different America, the one in the South, and this is its music." He sits on a buoy, places the bandoneon across his knees ("with his back to the audience, so the pretence does not seem too obvious") and while he moves his shoulders and arms to the music, from the orchestra pit we hear the strains of "Re Fa Si". Little by little the girls start to move to the rhythm of the music, and then from the depths of the liner an equal number of smartly dressed, very polite young men appear. They each take a girl by the hand and start to teach them the steps of this new dance. The curtain goes down on this ensemble.

Third scene: the male dancers of the previous act are all sitting round a table, which a spotlight picks out in the surrounding darkness. They are dressed in dinner jackets and are talking of sums of money which are not immediately recognisable: 2000 for lot six to Rosario, lot fourteen can be left for San Fernando. Then a second spotlight appears, and up on a platform we see the leading man from the previous scenes. He is no longer carrying a musical instrument, and no longer looks either melancholy or enthusiastic: this time he is in command, and sternly calls the others to pay attention. He presents a very young woman who is wearing only a transparent shift. The lights on stage come up, and we see we are in a large room that could be a night-club. There are more men at several tables; one of them gets up, goes over to the platform and lifts the girl's shift to get a good look at what's underneath. Another man opens her mouth with one hand to examine her teeth. All at once, she starts sobbing: the music swells up and her sobs turn into a song. It is the tune "From my Neighbourhood", with what the libretto calls "appropriate modifications": replacing "I was brought up in a convent" the girl sings "at home we always observed the *shabat*". There is a sudden change of tone when she reaches the verses that say: "Today I dance the tango, I'm mad about dancing, they call me crazy and who knows what else . . ." At this point the leading actor, who now is the master of ceremonies for the other procurers, embraces the young girl, who goes on singing ("I'm a flower in the mud, anybody's woman") and leads her in a dance. The watching men all applaud, the music repeats the theme a second time, this time without any words, and it grows in intensity until it reaches the final tableau, with all the dancers freezing on the spot.

The libretto states that at this point there is an interval. I also thought it was a good idea to have a break from my reading. I was astonished. This was not the first time that, to my annoyance, I confirmed that I had somehow acquired an awareness of what to me was acceptable or not, however hard I had tried to keep a distance from what today is known as "politically correct". I found myself wondering how it was possible for this musical comedy not only to be put on for an audience, but for it to have been fairly successful. I decided yet again that a humble approach was best. The script must tell me something about that audience and about the time when a work like that could be accepted without embarrassment. Perhaps the scenes to come would shed some light on it . . .

I hurried through the next act. The unfortunate girl is called Taube ("Dove"), and her rebellious nature means that she is very soon expelled from a luxurious establishment in Rosario (based on the one run by Madame Sapho?) where she was rechristened Yvette from Montmartre. She ends up in another place on Lavalle and Junín in Buenos Aires, only to find herself punished still further and sent to the desolate southern outpost of Tres Arroyos. She returns to the capital and eventually tries to kill the sordid madame who runs the new house she finds herself in, on Calle Viamonte.

In the third act, Mendele, her pimp, who by now has completely adapted to life in South America, saves her from jail by taking the blame for the failed murder attempt, and redeems himself by denouncing the sinister organisation he works for to the authorities. In jail, he evades the attempts at revenge carried out by his former colleagues, many of whom have also been arrested. His only consolation is the long line of girls who bring him cigarettes, warm socks, bottles of cologne, and home-made sweets. Taube is of course first in line, and she is the one who closes the show with the song: "Listen to your heart / if you're feeling lost / its voice will show the path / leading to redemption". The tune gradually becomes a two-four rhythm, the bars on Mendele's cell fall away as if by magic, and he, in shirt-sleeves and with unkempt hair, dances a tango with Taube. One by one, the other girls find a partner and start to dance as well, keeping a respectful distance from the main couple.

Underneath the words "Final Curtain" there is a note in pencil to the effect that if there should be an encore, the last tango song is not to be reprised, but all the company should come out on stage to dance Firpo's "Dawn".

NIGHTFALL CAME EARLY THAT WINTER AFTERNOON, OR
perhaps I had stayed longer than I intended in the basement
of the Cervantes Theatre, in that Theatre History Institute
which now, as I was crossing Avenida Córdoba on Calle
Libertad, seemed to me more like a dangerous crypt than a
cave full of unexpected treasure. Pursued by its unshakeable
phantoms, I walked past the synagogue guarded by
policemen who could not disguise their yawns, and headed
for the Colón Theatre. Questions were crowding in my mind,
impatient to receive the ambivalent answers I knew I was
unable to give. Who was the owner of that lost or perhaps
hidden libretto? The name did not figure in the card index
alongside its title. All that was included on the card index in
addition to *The Moldavian Pimp* was the date of its first performance at the Ombú Theatre.

I thought that perhaps this tiny clue might be pointing
me towards some newspaper collection, to see if there was
any reference to the show on that particular date. The newspaper library in the National Library was impossible: the

staff there had been on strike since time immemorial. As on other occasions, I had to turn to the library of the National Congress, whose convenient night-time opening hours had already been useful to me in the past. Some time after midnight that same day, after struggling to find a seat among pensioners snoozing over police reports from their youth ("Kid Ayerza Kidnapped", "Little Big Ears Strikes Again") and employees with their eyes half-closed as they sipped *maté* and clung to their thermoses for warmth, I discovered that neither *La Nación* nor *La Prensa* included Yiddish theatre in their lists of entertainment.

I had already decided to call it a day and was on my way out when I noticed an old fellow, who was either extremely short-sighted or who had fallen asleep, with his face plunged into the pages of a bound collection of the *Idishe Tseitung*, which seemed bigger than he was. I went over to him and saw that the newspaper was not just written in Yiddish, but had whole columns in Spanish, or at least in Latin characters. I was about to return more hopefully to the issue desk when this unlikely reader suddenly stirred and smiled a toothless but friendly smile at me.

"Did you want this volume?"

I assured him I did not want to deprive him of it, and took advantage of his friendly disposition to ask him if the newspaper had a list of plays being performed. I was taken aback to realise immediately that I had opened the floodgates: like a lot of "elderly" people, now that he had found someone to talk to, he was not going to give up the chance to say his piece. He rattled off a string of questions: what was I looking for, was it a particular theatre, perhaps I was interested in tours by Maurice Schwartz or Ben Ami, he could remember Alexander Moissi himself, had seen Molly Picon in *Oh! What a Girl!*, and to prove it he closed his eyes and started to hum, *Oy iz dos a meydl!* I could trust his memory: "I forget everything that happened last week, thank God, but you can rely on me for the important things. For example, I remember the Tragic Week in 1919, even though I was only ten years old at the time." Each phrase was punctuated by a metallic laugh that shook his false teeth but did nothing to stop the flow.

I'm not sure if it was a sudden intuition or simply the need to get a word in edgeways that led me to blurt out the year 1927, the name of the Ombú Theatre, and the title *The Moldavian Pimp*. He laughed so loudly he was in danger of waking the staff snoring nearby.

"I was there, in my first pair of long trousers. I can't remember now what excuse I gave my parents: they would have died if they'd known I was going to see a play like that . . ."

An anonymous shush! and a stern glance from a young woman reader suggested it might be best to continue our conversation outside the library. I invited the old man to have a drink in one of the late-night cafés on Avenida Entre Ríos. He responded enthusiastically, getting to his feet with surprising agility. He brushed a few unidentifiable crumbs from his lapels and said in a firm voice:

"Ariel Nisenson, at your service."

A few minutes later, seated at a table in the Café Quorum, after asking if it was all right to order a whisky, he stared out at the imposing Congress building. His nostalgic air seemed almost theatrical as he gazed at the metal barriers and the police guard around it. There were only a few passers-by scurrying along in the cold, and they seemed to pose no great threat either to the building or the institution.

"What is this place coming to? The representatives of the people have to defend themselves against the attacks of the people . . . well, I suppose it's no great surprise. This country has always lived on lies: they turned President Yrigoyen into an idol, but he didn't shrink from ordering people shot in Patagonia, or of looking the other way during the Tragic Week . . ."

I had a hard time persuading him to abandon his over-view of Argentine history, which might have been accurate but risked going on until dawn. Eventually I butted in and asked him a direct question: did he know who had written *The Moldavian Pimp*?

"Of course. Theo Auer. Did you ever meet him? No, of course not! You're too young. Auer must have died at the end of the fifties, I should think; it was before Eichmann was captured anyway . . . a crazy old guy; or perhaps not so crazy after all . . . there were lots of stories about him. Towards the end of his life he was a matchmaker, a *shatkes*, if you know what I mean. He would meet people every day at the Café León — it's not there any more — between Corrientes and Pueyrredón. But they said that in his younger days he had been a fine catch himself. Well anyway, of the dead nothing but good . . . Despite its success with the public, the community was against *The Moldavian Pimp*, at that time they were all up in arms over the question of Jewish pimps, the nationalists used the existence of the Zwi Migdal and 'Polish' girls for their anti-Jewish propaganda, as though the gangs from Marseilles and the 'Frenchies' weren't even more powerful. It's not that the play is in praise of prostitution, far from it, but it showed a pimp with feelings, capable of remorse, and kind-hearted girls . . . as you know, the Jewish community always adopted a policy of not creating a fuss, keeping *shtum*. A few days after the show was staged at the Ombú, they put pressure on for it to close. But the play continued, and on Calle Corrientes in the centre as well, in two theatres run by Mousey Gutman, who didn't seem worried about its theme . . . heaven knows why . . . In 1930, when the Zwi Migdal was broken up and the pimps fled to Montevideo or Rio de Janeiro, all the girls were left out on the street, and that wasn't better for anyone, I can tell you."

With difficulty, I tried to bring him round to what could possibly have been the link between this mysterious Theo Auer and the theme of the play: was he defending prostitution? Was he condemning it, but aiming completely wide

24

of the mark? Or was he reflecting the ambivalent feelings part of the public might have had regarding this particular theme? As I asked my questions I had the uncomfortable feeling I was imposing answers on him, but whenever I let the old man speak without directing him, he wandered off into his monologue on the political history of Argentina, in which Uriburu, Perón and other governments, civilian or military, all fused together to inspire a similar mistrust: "You youngsters have been brainwashed . . . Believe me, we haven't had a single decent government here since Alvear."

"Listen, I have only heard about Theo Auer, and as the tango says 'people are mean and like to gossip'. Why don't you go and see his daughter? She's still alive. She used to be the librarian at the Hatikva school until they forced her to retire, but last year she still went, on her sticks and every-thing, to the school's anniversary celebration. They must be able to give you her phone number."

By this time we were getting not so much impatient as weary looks from the people by the till. It was nearly three in the morning, a fine drizzle had started to fall, and ours was the only table occupied. I called the waiter over, and as I was paying him, Señor Nisenson offered me a final, sur-prising comment.

"How times change! Not long ago at this time of day in this café there were some good-looking women. What hap-pened to them? I wouldn't be surprised to find them in the bingo hall on Calle Rivadavia, and that shuts at six . . ."

4

"SO YOU'RE VISITING OLD FOLK . . . BE CAREFUL: IF AND when you're old yourself, you may find you're chasing after youngsters who won't even give you the time of day."

The woman studying me sarcastically was wrapped in a poncho and sat engulfed in a large armchair whose faded upholstery suggested it had once depicted hydrangeas on a dark-green background. Despite the yellowing strands of her hair and a complicated network of wrinkles, her hard-eyed gaze was level and unwavering. I had explained to her how I had discovered Theo Auer's name from *The Moldavian Pimp*, how I had come across that play during my research on Yiddish theatre in Buenos Aires, and I also told her about my meetings with Sami Warschauer and Ariel Nisenson. But none of this appeared to have made her any the less wary.

"Yiddish theatre is dead. It was something for poor immigrants, for a community that had no future. For good or ill – don't ask me which – they've all been integrated now. I don't know why you want to revive . . . all that."

I embarked on a short version of the speech I had given several times to my supervisor in the School of Journalism. I was reassured that at least she wasn't suspicious that someone she probably thought was a *goy* should be curious about the topic.

"Only a youngster who isn't a Jew could be interested in those out-of-date things. They were very basic productions, with actors who were at best amateur. All the public demanded was that they speak their language, a language that was already dying out, though they didn't realise it. And I'm talking about a time long before people studied Hebrew so they could emigrate to Israel: back in the twenties or thirties . . . Today thanks god, I don't think there's any trace left of Yiddish."

I didn't want to correct her impression, because behind her words I detected less a conviction than a sense of wishful thinking. When I arrived I had noticed a map of the state of Israel framed on the wall in the entrance to her apartment. Among the few objects relieving the austerity of her home, I paused in front of two photographs in Argentine silver frames: they were portraits of two people dressed apparently in nineteenth-century clothes. Without rising from her armchair, she pointed to one of them:

"My father, Teófilo Auerbach. He wasn't a man of the theatre, and towards the end of the life he used to get very annoyed if anyone mentioned this play to him, even though it was quite successful. That Warschauer fellow you spoke of upset him once by suggesting he put it on again; my father threw him out on his ear. He wasn't bothered about success, but he was put out that *The Moldavian Pimp* created confusion. Ah well, young people never think of the consequences of what they do."

I asked her if the woman in the other portrait was her mother. She laughed heartily.

"If only she had been! That's Bertha Pappenheim. Have you never heard of her? She was the pride of European Jewish women. At the turn of the twentieth century she set up organisations to fight against procurers, she even travelled to Eastern Europe to study the situation in the pale of settlement. I bet you don't know what that is either . . . the *Ansiedlungsrayon*, the area where the Russian empire permitted the Jews to settle, far from the big cities . . ."

I encouraged her to tell me more about Pappenheim and her activities. I knew nothing about them, but she obviously admired her tremendously.

"All you have to do is go to a library: get information, read the books. Oh, I know, you young people today have no idea what it means to go and search out information, you all have the internet at home . . . but beware, not everything floating through the air can be trusted. Anyway, just remember that it was Bertha Pappenheim who, with a courage none of the menfolk have shown either before or since, said that if so many poor Jewish girls had fallen into prostitution and were being ruthlessly exploited by pimps who were also Jewish, then the reason for it was to be found in the oppression women have suffered in our tradition. How else to explain the fact that those pimps were such believers, that they built their own synagogues and even cemeteries when they were expelled from the community? Right from the start, Jewish women were seen as unclean, *unsauber*; once they had 'fallen' they were nothing more than merchandise . . . even you must know that in traditional synagogues even 'wives and mothers' are kept separate, relegated to another floor. They're not allowed access to holy texts or to study. Which was a good thing: as soon as they did start to study and had the chance to get to university, they went straight to Marx and Engels rather than the Talmud. I hope you've heard of Rosa Luxemburg at least."

I took the risk of pointing out the contradiction between this admiration and the fact that in the entrance to her apartment (just like a *mezuza*, I thought, but chose not to demonstrate my knowledge of the tradition) she had a map of the state of Israel.

"You must come again so we can talk. Perhaps we'll get to know each other a little. You're a strange young man. Don't get me wrong: I mean you're out of the ordinary. But I don't want to talk about Israel. Just remember that Israel is one thing, and the Israelis something else. Like France: 'liberty equality, fraternity' – that's what she means to people of my generation. My father had Zola's portrait

29

hanging in his library all his life. Then there's the French, the ones who set such a shining example during the Occupation. But it's late, don't get me started again. Call me whenever you feel like it."

5

THERE IS SOMETHING PARTICULARLY OPPRESSIVE ABOUT winter evenings in Buenos Aires. The dwindling light and dankness of empty Sunday afternoons seem like an invitation to seek refuge in an obsession. Some people discover the possibility of love, of whispered caresses, bodies mingling between four walls, warm sheets, before they emerge into the night. Others seek out parallel lives in novels or the cinema. I have to admit I'm too timid for the former, which I have only very occasionally tried, and without much success, and too demanding for the latter means of escape, which only succeeds in capturing my imagination for a short while, and leaves me with a lingering feeling of dissatisfaction.

Sometimes I wonder if it wasn't to escape those empty Sundays that I threw myself so recklessly into this unexpected detour I had stumbled across while researching something at first linked to my studies but which quickly took on a life of its own. To me, the characters and situations it offered were far more novelistic than anything I could find in printed fiction. My supervisor asked me ironically how my investigation was going. He did not realise that this word from the police world fitted my behaviour exactly: the fact was, I was no longer reading history books, but poring over old newspapers and theatre programmes, and visiting people whose evasive or partial answers I collated each night on the screen of my Mac. I was building up descriptions of people and places on its illuminated rectangle: a dense real-life drama I was trying to penetrate and participate in. It was a way of rescuing me from my "two-room" apartment in Colegiales, where the only trace of the past was a set of china I had never used and had stashed at the back of a cupboard. Neither my mother nor father had wanted to keep it when they separated, presumably because it reminded them of a marriage they preferred to forget.

This was how I began to learn of the Zwi Migdal, the "shadowy organisation" and its precursors, "mutual aid" societies like the Varsovia or the Asquenasum, with their alternative cemeteries and their hidden synagogues at Córdoba 3280 in Buenos Aires or Güemes 2965 in Rosario. I also began to learn about how the Jewish community had fought back – the posters the writer Robert Arlt had seen: "pimps will not be served" in shops, and "no entry for pimps" in the theatres; the countless lawsuits taken out by girls fleeing from brothels: lawsuits always rejected by judges, prosecutors, police chiefs and ordinary policemen, all of them irreproachable Christians, all of them bribed by the secret organisation. I learnt about Raquel Liberman, whose entire savings they said had been lost in the 1929 Wall Street crash, and when she protested, threatened at first to cut her face and then with something far worse if she continued to complain. I read about Judge Rodríguez Ocampo, who listened to her, protected her, and put on trial 108 members of the Zwi Migdal who had not escaped Argentina thanks to the passports sold them by police chief Eduardo Santiago.

But these silhouettes and stories only served to support my search for others, the ones related to the area of show business from which I had started out. I am afraid that somewhere deep down I was still the adolescent who follows interesting looking strangers in the street to see where they are going, whom they meet, where they live, and who on more than one occasion has been accosted by these all-too-real people, reacting indignantly or simply in bewilderment before he managed to transform them into fiction.

There really was little difference between that and the imaginative effort I employed on the scraps reality offered me, starting to weave a fiction around the existence of characters I had no more information about than a few names and dates, inventing their stories on the basis of mere glimpses of situations . . .

PART TWO

I

ON SOME SPRING NIGHTS THE SMELL OF THE SEA REACHES
Tres Arroyos. People say the sound of the waves is also carried on the wind, but to me that seems pure fantasy. The
tang of salt on the cool breeze that relieves the first heat
of approaching summer: I can believe that. But that is all.
During the month of October 1931, in a beaten earth patio
under the eaves of a tiled roof, at a time when the fumes
from the few passing trucks were not enough to obliterate
the faint smell, and the ubiquitous murmur of invisible
televisions was not yet to be heard, it is possible that the
attention of the young girl sitting in her rocking-chair
between tubs of hydrangea and geraniums could for a
moment have been aroused by this herald of a new season.

She has a shawl across her knees. She brought it to cover
her shoulders, because she is only wearing a thin cotton
nightdress, but once she was out on the patio she decided to
fold it in her lap and enjoy this fresh breeze wafting through
the warm air. Inside she has left the smell of stale rooms,
cigarette smoke, and disinfectant. She knows it will not be

long before Doña Carmen's voice calls her in. (Doña Carmen, whose real name is Feigele Szuster, and who struggles to pronounce the "r" in the name she has been given.) But she has learnt that peace, which some call happiness and others pleasure, is not measured by how long it lasts, but by the intensity of the always fleeting moment in which it visits us. And tonight Doña Carmen is going to be busy a good while: Kloter Leille has come for the monthly inspection, and the two of them are closeted together going over the accounts.

The girl is nineteen years old, but does not know it: she has no idea of when or where she was born. She arrived in Argentina with a folded piece of paper, worn at the edges: on it was a lot of writing she did not know how to read, as well as the portrait a travelling photographer took of her in her village. It did not look much like her. But when she arrived the piece of paper (which during her journey she had sewn into her petticoat lining) ended up in the hands of a man whose name she did not understand, and then was passed from one madame to another. It is Doña Carmen who has it now, together with other similar pieces of paper known as passports that belong to the other girls. She keeps them all in a tobacco-coloured file with white patches that she calls "calf-skin" and keeps in the top drawer of her desk, which she locks.

The girl can only write one word: her name, Zsuzsa. (Back in her village it was pronounced Djudya; when she reached Buenos Aires she was taught to say it like Susana.)

A big ship took her from Trieste to Montevideo, then a much smaller one brought her and another five girls across the River Plate, on such a clear night they could count all the stars and discover their new shapes in the southern sky. She never saw the other girls again. The prettiest among them were taken to a city called Rosario; the others stayed in Buenos Aires. She got through the questions at immigration thanks to the man whose name she never understood, but who seemed to command the officials' respect when he spoke to them in Spanish. He told the girls, in a mixture of Russian and Yiddish, that to speed things up they should say they were his or his wife's nieces.

It is two years since she passed through immigration, and among the first words she learnt in her new country were "steamship of the line" and the name "Mihanovich", which together with "thank you" were constantly on the lips of their unknown host. All that is just a vague memory now. In those days she had clean hands; now when she looks down, she sees her fingers are dyed a reddish purple colour, and knows that however hard she scrubs them with Marseilles soap she will never get rid of the stains of potassium permanganate with which she washes her clients' penis and testicles. It was precisely because "she hurt" one of them that her wandering life began. She was sent from Señora Rifka's house in Calle Paso to the place old man Srul ran in Calle Tucumán. There, she had picked up and kept some banknotes that had fallen from a client's pocket, but he had noticed and informed the brothel-keeper.

That was how she ended up being punished with the other girls in one of Kloter Leille's places. She had made friends with a young blonde girl who spent the whole day singing tangos. Her name was Esther, she knew she had been born in Romania seventeen years earlier, and boasted that she had been in twelve brothels before being sent to Tres Arroyos for biting several clients "down there". The two girls often slept in each other's arms, and although Doña Carmen did not like the idea ("No funny business here") she permitted them these brief moments of tenderness and even affection, because they did not interfere with their work. How old was Doña Carmen? Esther said she must be over seventy, but Zsuzsa could not even imagine anyone that ancient. She looks older than the image she keeps in her memory of her mother . . . whatever the truth, she is not helped by her elaborate make-up or a wavy hairstyle that ends with curls over ears that are as huge as all old people's are.

Esther has also told her that Doña Carmen spent several months in jail. After she had retired from the game, she had tried to "set up on her own". She began taking a small Pekinese dog wearing a smart tweed coat for a walk every day round Plaza Lavalle. A plainclothes policeman who had seen her there on several afternoons finally decided to confront her one October day when the spring warmth made the animal's attire seem particularly incongruous. After smiling and patting the suffering Peke, he thrust his hand under the woollen coat and pulled out several packets of cocaine. These, rather than any erotic services, were what Feigele was offering her new clients. A few months later, by now known as Carmen, which Leille thought more appropriate for the "southern frontier", Feigele left Buen Pastor prison and had to accept being moved to Tres Arroyos.

Zsuzsa has no idea what tweed might be, and the name Plaza Lavalle does not conjure up any image for her. The word "cocaine", though, makes her laugh, just as she laughed when a client in the Calle Paso house put some up her nose before penetrating her. In Tres Arroyos, Doña Carmen reserves it for the musicians who on Saturday nights play tangos on this same patio where Zsuzsa now sits sighing, eyes closed, as if trying to keep the faintly salty breeze as long as possible in her lungs. At the end of those Saturday nights, when the last clients are leaving, the musicians play softly for themselves, not so that the others can dance. That is when their instruments: the bandoneon, the guitar and the violin, appear to change register; it's as though they are singing or talking.

Zsuzsa loves to listen to them. It's almost time to go to bed until noon the following day, and she already knows that tonight she will not be sleeping alone, or protected by little Esther's chaste embrace. The bandoneon player is murmuring more than singing:

"Hey sweetheart listen,
to the melody of my sad bandoneon,
hey sweetheart listen,
to my poor heart's anxious beating,
hey sweetheart listen,
to far-off landscapes this tango conjures for you . . ."

The musician is called Samuel Warschauer, and he is obviously very young. For the price of a single session, Doña Carmen lets him stay in Zsuzsa's bed all night. The next morning, he has coffee with the others at the big table, then leaves without a word until the following Saturday. Bertha, the oldest whore in the house, who is always enveloped in the sharp smell of ether, never fails to choose that moment to tell Zsuzsa with a mocking smile and a strong Polish accent: "one of these Saturdays, he won't be back".

Zsuzsa knows that. What she doesn't know, because she has never read a novel, is that she is in love. She does realise though that the musician has "a crush" on her. For the first few nights he used her just like any other client, then fell fast asleep beside her. Soon though, he began to take his time, to caress her, to show her what a man's hand can arouse in a woman's nipples or between her legs, however much use they have been put to. Once he even made as if to kiss her.

But above all he gradually began to talk. At first he talked about the other places he played in, in Bahía Blanca, Coronel Pringles, Ingeniero White. Later on, he began talking about himself. Sometimes Zsuzsa does not understand everything he is saying, but she realises he does not open up like this to every girl. She learns that Samuel was born in Buenos Aires, and that it was his parents who came from overseas. They have a mattress shop in Paternal, and threw him out when he learnt to play the bandoneon rather than the violin, for which his father was paying for lessons. "Bandoneon is tango, and tango is lowlife." Samuel laughs at this, but Zsuzsa can see the hurt in his eyes when he repeats this phrase spoken by a father who despite being almost deaf had so much respect for music, especially for the violin which, although he could hardly hear it, he knew to be the only instrument any decent Jewish boy should play. (In Tarnopol, where he was an apprentice in his grandfather's workshop, he had pierced his right eardrum with a mattress-maker's needle to avoid compulsory conscription into the Imperial army.)

Esther has told Zsuzsa not to build up any hopes: she has no right to dream that Samuel will buy her and carry her off far away . . . far away from where? Zsuzsa had never even thought about it, but now her companion has mentioned this impossible dream, an unimaginable possibility starts to raise its timid head. What was there beyond the walls of the different houses she had inhabited? Back in the old country she had only known a village with earthen streets, then at thirteen she had been handed over to the landlord with a kiss on the forehead from her parents, who owed many months' rent. In this new country, everything was different. The men smelt of cigarettes, of beer and carbolic soap, not of ingrained sweat on their shirts, dried cow dung on the soles of their shoes.

One Monday afternoon, when she was still in Buenos Aires, Señora Rifka had taken the girls for an outing to Palermo in an open carriage. In the park Zsuzsa had seen neat gardens, an artificial lake and children dressed in white. These were visions she could not relate to in any way: they were no more than images (although they were moving ones) like those she had seen in *Caras y Caretas* or *El Hogar*, old copies of which were left by Doña Carmen on the low table in the brothel waiting-room, although none of the men ever glanced at them. Samuel also seems to her to come from some unbelievable world, completely different from anything she knew, a world promised more by the music of the tangos than by their words, which she still only half understands.

Almost an hour has gone by, and nobody has called her. All of a sudden, she is worried. What if clients have arrived and chosen other girls? What if she doesn't collect enough tokens tonight to avoid being punished by Doña Carmen? She looks in at the kitchen window and sees Pancha, who was once called Pancho. She is busy with what she calls her daily miracle: making an acceptable stew from all the leftovers. Zsuzsa waves and lifts her chin to query him. "Nobody, Yuyita, nobody; don't worry, I'll tell you if any clients arrive," Pancha whispers with a beaming smile. "The boss is still doing the accounts," she says, and blows the young girl a kiss before returning to her stew. Zsuzsa is very fond of Pancha: as well as doing the cooking, she cuts and combs their hair, washes and irons their nightdresses, and half-heartedly dusts and sweeps their rooms. She worked for many years in a house in Ensenada as a "special attraction" until increasing age forced her to change her line of work, but not her surroundings. Even Doña Carmen has to laugh when she tells them some of her stock of anecdotes.

Zsuzsa is about to return to her rocking-chair in the patio when she hears a strange noise. She does not recognise it as coming from a car which has pulled up a hundred metres away but whose engine has been left running. She cannot see it because the back wall is in the way, but the muffled roar reminds her of another sound, the one that every Saturday announces the arrival of the musicians to a chorus of laughter and shouts. The gate opens and in the darkness she recognises – but isn't this Tuesday, so what is he doing here? – Samuel. He rushes over to her, whispers that there's no time to lose, puts his arm round her waist and drags her in her nightdress and shoeless out of the patio and into the street, where Doña Carmen has forbidden them to go. But Samuel forces her to run with him to the Chevrolet parked on the next block, ready for a quick getaway. Behind the wheel she sees Marcos, the violinist, and he immediately puts the car in gear, drives round the corner, and speeds off along a track that seems invisible in the gloom.

Zsuzsa has no idea where they are taking her. The salty breeze is blowing strongly that October night, and I am sure she can feel her heart beat as loudly as the sound of the distant waves she has never heard in Tres Arroyos.

2

OFTEN, MANY MONTHS LATER, ZSUZSA WOULD RECALL that night: the salty breeze on her face, Samuel's protective arm and the unknown thrill his embrace aroused in her. It was a mixture of a tranquil kind of curiosity as to what might await her at the end of this journey, combined with a complete lack of concern about it, as if there were nothing beyond his embrace and the darkness rushing by outside the car windows. That was suddenly all that existed for her, barefoot in her cotton nightdress, curled up beside this musician with whom she had slept on so many Saturday nights, this man she had allowed to use her like any other client, until one morning for the first time in her life he had given her pleasure, had helped her discover that moment of absence, or fullness, which she does not know is called orgasm, something she never imagined a man could offer a woman.

In a room in a boarding-house in Ingeniero White, Zsuzsa (who by now has accepted the name of Susana) is waiting for Samuel. She is sitting at the window, flicking through a copy of *Vosotras*. She cannot read it, but enjoys looking at the illustrations. From the street come the jumbled sounds of the nearby port: voices, an occasional shout in an unknown language, the lumbering manoeuvre of a ship leaving or tying up at a wharf, and beyond that the distant rumble of a train at the far end of Calle Cárrega, under the La Niña de Hierro bridge. She is sick; she coughs, but has no idea of the name of the illness that will put an end to her short life only a few weeks later. She is not growing impatient: she never knows when Samuel will be coming back, but he always brings something to eat and a consoling bottle. He also caresses her just as he did the first time she felt pleasure, even though Zsuzsa tires quickly now and can no longer reach that moment of blind oblivion, that lightning flash in the darkness that she discovered in Tres Arroyos, and which bound her to this man for ever. She is happy with the memory of pleasure: it wipes out the boarding-house room, the damp patches on the walls, the smell of frying that seeps through all the cracks.

Samuel tells her everything. He's still playing the bandoneon, but no longer in the houses of ill-repute of the town and region. Local impresarios have noticed him, and he is now part of the Milongueros del Sur orchestra, performing at carnival dances and with invitations from as far away as Viedma and Carmen de Patagones. He's also met a woman, Perl Rust, who two years earlier had escaped on foot from a house in Granadero Baigorria in Santa Fe

48

province. The members of the orchestra are protecting her in this distant south. She is no longer being searched for by Zacharías Zitnitzky's men: following the 1930 police raids, he has been forced to escape across the River Plate to Montevideo, thanks to a fake passport Inspector Santiago obtained for him. Nor is she being threatened with having to return to Rosario or having her face cut, or being forced to work evenings in one of the curtained-off boxes in the Alhambra cinema. She has a good voice and sings tangos with the orchestra.

Zsuzsa realises that Samuel likes Perl, but chooses to believe he does not love the newcomer more than her. She dimly understands that pity can be a complex feeling, stronger and less direct than love, and so feels sure that Samuel will not leave her in the state she is in, "sick and penniless". Besides which, Perl does not just sing: she still works for herself, and hands over part of her earnings to Samuel. Thanks to this, he can provide Zsuzsa with a few treats.

Zsuzsa does not want to know what Perl looks like. It's obvious that Samuel is careful not to say too much about her: he once remarked that she was the orchestra's singer and that he liked her. On another occasion he mentioned she had "got him out of a spot" by lending him some money; Zsuzsa knows what that means, and although she isn't too bothered about the gesture itself, she realises that her days have become numbered. Some evenings she starts to cry, and cannot stop. Although she would not be able to explain why this happens, in her mind's eye she sees the image of her own face as she so often catches it in the wardrobe mirror — her sunken cheeks, the way that her make-up, rather than disguising her ill-health, makes her look old before her time. Then by contrast she imagines a young, fresh face whose imprecise features change constantly, but which undeniably belongs to Perl, that woman who can still work as she cannot, and who gives Samuel the money she earns.

Tonight Samuel arrives shortly before nine. He's brought a bottle of liquor, at the bottom of which float hundreds of golden particles. They look like flakes of gold, and the label in fact boasts that this is *Danziger Goldwasser*. The two of them laugh as they hold the bottle up against the turquoise-coloured tulip bedside light, shake it gently and watch as the specks of fool's gold rise, twist and turn, then fall back to the bottom of the bottle. What if they were real gold? Samuel was given it by a Polish ship's captain who loves tango and who the previous night had danced till dawn in Los Tres Hemisferios, where the Milongueros del Sur are appearing at the moment. The orchestra had already packed up and only Samuel agreed to continue playing while the captain went on with his intense, tireless practice of steps and twirls, followed by two sleep-walking partners.

Tonight Samuel is going back, to play until heaven knows

what hour. Zsuzsa knows what that means: he'll eat a few slices of sausage on rye bread with her, toss down two or three glasses of genever, then caress her until she falls asleep and he can leave for work with a clear conscience. But this time, Zsuzsa only pretends to be sleeping. She realises that Samuel's caresses, which had once seemed to her a privilege only she was worthy of, have now become a subterfuge: he is saving his energy for later, in Perl's bed.

Samuel has gone. Zsuzsa finds herself alone again. She is no longer coughing, but feels feverish, and presses her legs together under her nightdress, as if to relieve a stinging pain that may not be physical. All of a sudden she has an urge to be possessed, not to be caressed and spoken to gently, or even gently penetrated. She wants to be so exhausted she could die; she wants to be worn out the way she used to be when the clients queued to have her, a new one every ten or fifteen minutes, so quickly that she hardly had time to carry out the hygienic ritual she had learnt almost as soon as she had landed in Buenos Aires. She stares down at her pale fingers, where there is still a faint trace of the reddish purple colour no soap has ever been able to wash away, and senses a strength that was not there minutes earlier. She gets up and wraps her woollen coat – the only warm clothing she has – round her shoulders. Out of her two pairs of shoes she chooses the almost new ones. They are pearl-grey and have high heels, and she puts them on without any stockings. She sprinkles toilet water on the front of her nightdress, all that's left from the bottle Samuel gave her the day they arrived at the boarding-house, "the start of a new life". Before she leaves the room she takes a look at herself in the mirror, but turns away quickly so as not to see her feverish eyes and smudged make-up.

The port of Bahía Blanca is called Ingeniero White, and both English and Spanish express that lack of colour which astonished the first travellers when they caught sight of the vast saltpetre flats, only occasionally interrupted by mud pools full of crabs. Through the cold June mist, which the pale streetlights tinge with a yellow hue, I can see a woman's unsteady figure. Zsuzsa is stumbling down streets that lead to the docks, across railway sidings that run from the station to individual warehouses whose names figure on tall zinc roofs: Drysdale, Dreyfus, Bunge y Born. She does not know where to find what she is looking for; perhaps she rushes on without knowing exactly what she is looking for. Whatever it is, it is not a man, although a man helped her put an end to this nameless anxiety gnawing at her.

They are building new wharves and grain silos. Labourers from Patagonia and Chile have come to Ingeniero White to work alongside European immigrants. Zsuzsa passes some of them on her way to the port, and they quickly look the other way, just as she had done when she saw her reflection in the wardrobe mirror. Far from humiliating her, this sign of rejection only gives her renewed strength. She pauses for a moment outside the steamed-up window of the Salonika bar, where Greek sailors are dancing, their arms round each other's shoulders. In the distance she sees a neon sign and can read the letters which make up the words Los Tres Hemisferios; no longer hesitating, she sets off again resolutely towards it.

Is Perl that woman dressed in red who is singing "The Circus Girl" for an inattentive public? She is older than Zsuzsa, but has an energy about her that is very different from her own fever: her black eyes show determination, rage even, and the expressions she uses while she sings completely transform her. Among the musicians behind her, Zsuzsa spots Samuel, who apparently only has eyes for his bandoneon, which is resting across his knees on a spangled cloth. The trousers are an old pair she has darned for him on the inside of the leg: the orchestra only provides him with the dinner jacket, and that is shiny more from use than any pretensions of elegance its cloth might have, or the white shirt and black bow-tie. Do they lend Perl her red dress as well? It has a plunging v-shaped neckline, and her skirt has a slit up the side which gives occasional glimpses of her fish-net stockings. Perl's voice is warm, and she does not use the harsh notes or lisp that other tango singers cultivate. Zsuzsa cannot understand what she is singing, but feels the words must convey deep emotions, and that those emotions seem to belong to the woman herself. Who knows, if she understood the words, perhaps she would discover that they were the emotions she too felt.

Zsuzsa has taken a seat at a table. She does not see the owner signalling from behind the till to the waiter not to offer her anything. She does not call him over either. A crazy woman with feverish eyes, sunken cheeks and make-up all over the place, wearing a nightdress under a mousy coat: not the sort of customer they want in this dance-hall, even if its ambitions are no grander than seeking to attract a few night-owls who want to dance or get at the women, without arousing the suspicions of the police. Zsuzsa waits for Samuel to spot her, to lift his gaze from the instrument whose keys he is caressing, and which he suddenly swoops low over, or seems at times to be playing with as if it were a child. Eventually their eyes meet. He does not smile, and the shadow that flits across his face tells Zsuzsa beyond any doubt that her presence there fills him with both shame and apprehension.

Perl finishes her song. A few men in the audience applaud, the orchestra takes a break, and while the other musicians climb down from their podium to sit at tables and drink genever, Samuel pretends he is adjusting the bandoneon pleats, looking for a score: anything to put off the moment when he has to acknowledge Zsuzsa's presence, to go over and exchange at least a few words with her. Zsuzsa can see Perl waiting at a table for two, watching Samuel's pointless activity without understanding what he is up to, and she understands it would be better for her to leave, to return to the boarding-house even though she has no idea where it is or how to reach it. As she emerges into the street the cold wind hits her and she starts coughing once more. She leans against the wall and spits onto the pavement. The red blob slides slowly into the gutter.

This is the last time that Zsuzsa sets foot outside the boarding-house. A fortnight later she is carried out to be interned in the ward for infectious diseases at the City Hospital. She dies there before the return of spring. Samuel spends every evening at her bedside; he has given up the chance to tour with the Milongueros del Sur to Tandil and even Mar del Plata. When he is with her he is very careful not to mention Perl's name. He takes her bottles of toilet water and brightly coloured handkerchiefs, and when the nurse is not doing her rounds and the other patients appear to be sleeping, he caresses her in the place she likes so much, even though she can hardly feel anything now.

More than the doctors' euphemisms and Samuel's sad smile, it is this absence of sensation that convinces Zsuzsa her life is draining away. The peeling walls, the damp patches on the ceiling where she sees the same faces as on those at the boarding-house, the smell of the paraffin heaters that is not disguised by the eucalyptus leaves bubbling in saucepans on top of them: as the days drift by, as the hours sometimes seem endless, and as others rush past, all this blurs into one. At some point she again becomes the little girl running along a dirt track lined with acacias and linden trees. She plunges into the cool grass and rolls and rolls until she has lost her breath, in a country whose name has changed as the borders have shifted, and lies there trying to imagine the unimaginable world awaiting her on the far side of the ocean.

3

IT WAS PERL WHO FIRST BEGAN CALLING SAMUEL SAMI.

She realised she was lost from the start if she had dared say anything about Zsuzsa, if she so much as referred to her sick colleague shut up in her boarding-house room. Perl knew Zsuzsa was as present in Samuel's thoughts as she herself was absent from his shared secrets, that Zsuzsa had the terrible power of the unspoken. Perl quickly saw that the role Samuel assigned her as shoulder to cry on, accomplice, as well as physical relief and comfort, could be an investment for the future. It was Marcos, the orchestra's violinist, who had told her of Zsuzsa's existence and had confided that she did not have long to live. Perl decided to await the inevitable outcome with dignity and devotion, confident that this would make Sami hers completely. Perl knew intuitively he was the man who could get her out of Ingeniero White and Bahía Blanca, perhaps even take her to Buenos Aires with a new name.

In the early hours, when all the lights of Los Tres Hemisferios had been switched off, Perl gave herself to

Samuel in her first-floor room. She gasped and whispered words of love, and in the final spasm thrust her pelvis forward in an almost spontaneous gesture she had learnt to keep for her most generous clients. But she was not thinking of them: she had forgotten the years wasted in Granadero Baigorria. In a sincere surrender to Sami's pleasure, her unfeeling body mimicked the pleasure she could not experience. She watched him writhing between her legs and on her breasts until he reached the convulsion that left him trembling like a baby, ready to fall fast asleep at her side. As though caressing him, before enfolding Sami in a maternal embrace, Perl would gently remove his sheath and throw it into the chamber-pot under the bed.

She did not accompany him to the Jewish part of Ingeniero White cemetery, a narrow plot of land whipped by a wind that was filled less with the salty tang of the sea than the smell of rusty hulks or the oil from cargo boats going in and out of the port. Again, it was Marcos who described for her the numbered tomb along one of the side paths, the granite headstone with the name engraved on it: not Zsuzsa or Susana, but simply Yuya. There was no family name or date of birth, and the only inscription read: "Left Samuel on 4th September 1934".

That night, before Samuel went onto the podium to play in Los Tres Hemisferios, Perl embraced him silently and gave him a lengthy kiss of the sort she never usually offered him at that time and in that particular place. He let himself be kissed, and gave a faint smile before going out to perform and ask his colleagues in the orchestra to start with "To the Great Doll", a tune they did not normally include in their repertoire. While she waited for her turn to go on and sing, Perl watched as he played with a concentration she had rarely seen in him. In the corridor next to the podium where they had their improvised dressing-rooms surrounded by a jumble of cleaning implements and beer crates, Perl took a good look at herself in a badly-lit mirror. Its worn surface could not hide the harshness her features had acquired from the years of plying her trade.

For what seemed like an endless moment, she remembered the dressmaker's on Calle Paso where Recha Klatschmann had taken her in after her flight from Granadero Baigorria, how the heating was only put on whenever they had a client, and how the three girls had quickly to pick up their needles, thread and embroidery if the hygiene insepctors suddenly burst in to investigate the reports they had heard about the place, while any client had to escape out of the tradesmen's entrance, hastily doing up his trousers. She also recalled her earlier lessons in submission in Santa Fe, and before that the Steamship of the Line, and much earlier still, all the hopes and illusions she had felt when she boarded ship in a Black Sea port, one of the many young girls brought to Argentina by Señora de Zabladovich. (The same woman she was astonished to see in a September 1930 photograph in *Caras y Caretas*, looking haughty and wrapped in furs as she arrived at court to give evidence as "Emma the Millionairess"!) From this moment outside time, Perl slowly returned to Los Tres Hemisferios, and knew there was no doubt about it: Samuel had to become Sami, and the sooner the better.

She had understood that like so many men Sami was a romantic. She, like so many women, knew she was practical, level-headed, sensible. She would never be able to take the place in Sami's imagination of a tragic, unfortunate creature like Zsuzsa, so her modest but by no means simple plan was to make herself indispensable to her man's daily life. She saw her mission as being to rid Sami of his susceptibility to pathos, to rescue him from the tango. Perhaps thanks to him she would be able to achieve the uneventful existence she had longed for without really believing it possible, ever since those distant days when she had left her youth and credulity in the Granadero Baigorria brothel.

One winter night a stocky, bald man from Buenos Aires appeared at Los Tres Hemisferios. He had bushy eyebrows, rimless glasses, and smoked using an elegant cigarette holder. After listening to Sami play and Perl sing, he approached them with a politeness they were unused to. He turned out to be the famous orchestra leader Pancho Lomuto, whose greatest hit "The Tease" Perl had sung only a few minutes earlier. He was touring the province, and a musician replacing a sick violinist for one night – a local man who had played with Di Sarli before the later to be famous bandleader had left for the capital — had aroused the visitor's curiosity when he mentioned that in one of the bars in Ingeniero White there was a group of musicians who performed several of the tunes he had composed, including "Rebel Woman" and "The Moaner". During their brief conversation, Lomuto invited Sami and Perl to his table at the Hotel de Londres, in the centre of Bahía Blanca, the next day.

An experienced man of the world, this bandleader from the capital soon put them at their ease in what for them were surroundings they could only dream of. He told them about the cruises to Brazil or Tierra del Fuego on which his first orchestra had played, made them laugh with the story of a confused Englishwoman who had mistaken the cruise ship's destination and reached the Straits of Magellan swathed in tulle and muslin. When he took his leave, he encouraged them to try their luck in the capital. One of his friends was an impresario who put on shows in Yiddish at the Soleil and the Excelsior. If they spoke the language, that could help them take their first steps in the Buenos Aires showbusiness jungle.

Taking this in their stride, Sami and Perl said goodbye to him, the Hotel de Londres mirrors and the chandeliers reflected in them, its champagne and elegant manners. They took a tram back through the cold afternoon to Ingeniero White and their room on the first floor of Los Tres

Hemisferios. Sami voiced some doubts, but in her mind Perl had already begun to pack the light suitcases they would take with them to their new destination. They were bound to succeed: she could sing in both Yiddish and Spanish, and he had much more experience than the musicians who usually performed in that kind of theatre. Sami cautioned her that life in a big city could be daunting: he had read in the newspapers about the attacks nationalist groups had made on the cinemas showing *The House of Rothschild*, a Fox production, and even on the Teatro Cómico, where they had several times thrown gas bombs and interrupted performances of *The Races of Man*, the work of an Austrian author by the name of Ferdinand Bruckner, whom Sami had never suspected might be Jewish. Perl replied that these things happened because the Jews would not stay in their own neighbourhoods and insisted on going into the centre. Sami said nothing: he was secretly afraid that one night his parents might be in the stalls of one of those theatres in which he still could not believe he might be playing and perhaps even singing.

A week later the two of them auditioned for the secretary of the director of the Soleil Theatre in Buenos Aires. Perl sang "Papirosen" in Yiddish and "The Joker" in Spanish; Sami excelled himself yet again with "The Marne". Visibly impressed, the impresario offered to start them off at a modest wage, but with free lodgings in an apartment round the corner from the Excelsior Theatre. He also suggested they make their debut with the revue company, which was going to put on a show in a few weeks' time, between two seasons of "serious" theatre. He said he couldn't promise them more work in the Soleil, "because the public there is very demanding", but that he was sure there would be other worthwhile opportunities. The impresario was called Rubén; they did not quite catch whether his surname was Pasternak or Pustelnak. He never stopped smiling, wore a ring with a big red stone on his left ring-finger, and gave off abundant wafts of cologne. He was careful to look at them both during the audition, but his gaze lingered on Perl, and when they said goodbye he gripped her hand tightly.

Once installed in the Calle Malabia apartment, their lives soon took on a daily routine. Samuel would sleep until the afternoon. Perl would go out "to do the shopping" at around eleven and spend some time in Rubén's office. Samuel knew about, or perhaps only suspected, this tacit agreement which meant they avoided paying rent: it is possible that in secret it flattered his vanity as a man who had lived the tango for so long to have a woman who was no longer young but could still earn her keep.

The years rolled by. Kind-hearted Rubén preferred not to ask them for any rent even though he had long since waived the pleasure of Perl's daily visits. For his part Samuel, who by now was used to being called Sami, said nothing when Rubén was late paying their wages whenever

63

a surface crisis disturbed the tranquil waters of President Justo's government. At Lomuto's suggestion, Perl had begun to appear under the name of Perla Ritz, and soon achieved success thanks to this modest change from Rust, the family name the immigration officials had given her when she disembarked from the Ukraine. The audiences at the Excelsior and Soleil knew Sami less as a musician than as a compère. He would also sing a few songs, and became known as "the Yiddish Juan Carlos Thorry", a popular entertainer he vaguely resembled. Perl sang mostly in Yiddish, with occasional renditions in Spanish of tunes like "Granada" or "La pulpera de Santa Lucía". Even though there was no questioning her success, it did not spread beyond the invisible but strictly defined boundaries of the Abasto and Villa Crespo neighbourhoods.

4

PERL KNEW THAT ZSUZSA WAS IN THEIR CALLE
Malabia apartment.

Her invisible presence, with its faint perfume of eucalyptus, the "smell of the sick-room", clung to the overpowering wallpaper of geometric shapes and pastel colours (which Rubén had praised as an example of the most fashionable art deco when he first showed them round the apartment). It threw a long shadow across the bed where Sami and she now slept without touching one another. Neither the glass of water with cumin seeds in it that she put out on the balcony, nor the rubber plant with the absent woman's name written on a piece of paper tied to its roots, nor the thin strips of Indian paper she burnt in the ashtrays succeeded in dispelling this ghost, whom perhaps only Perl could see. She searched frantically in Sami's drawers for a photograph, ring, or handkerchief that she could cast out of the apartment to allow fresh air into her new life and set her man's thoughts free.

Another war had begun in Europe, and the Buenos Aires

audiences, even those made up of the most timid Jewish middle classes who followed the Yiddish theatre seasons, seemed gripped by a sense of affirmation or resistance. They laughed out loud, became emotional without shedding a tear, and carried on going to the theatre despite the appearance of nationalist tracts like *Pampero* and *Clarinada* for sale in the streets outside. As Perl watched Sami playing the accordion, even on the sought-after stage of the Soleil, she could tell from his fixed smile and absent gaze how humiliated he felt not to have a bandoneon across his knees, how sad he looked at having to devote his efforts to making something of "A bisale glik" or "Ale Farloin" rather than being able to give himself entirely to tangos like "Bygone Days" or "The Ninth of July". Even when Sami became the conductor of the Soleil's regular orchestra – a makeshift group of badly tuned violins, an almost inaudible double-bass and a squeaky clarinet – Perl knew that what she saw as their moment of triumph was not enough to make Sami forget the nostalgia he felt for the long nights in Los Tres Hemisferios, the misfortunes and uncertainties, the sheer wretchedness of his life in those days, which he clung on to as one does the first clumsy torments of love.

One evening Perl was left in the dressing-room looking for a pair of stockings that were not where she thought she had put them. Thinking there was no one else in the theatre by now apart from the night-watchman, she was crossing the stalls dimly lit by the light from streetlamps filtering in through an open door, when she heard the unmistakable sounds of a bandoneon. Up in a box, illuminated only by a dusty beam of light, she could see the outline of a figure hunched over the instrument, the hands nervous and alert as they alternately pressured and caressed the keys. This was Samuel, not Sami, and he was playing "My Life". She left the theatre at once and hurried back to their apartment.

When Sami returned half an hour later she pretended to be asleep, then waited until he really was sleeping to go and look in his bandoneon case for something that was not the instrument. She had no precise idea what she was looking for, but knew that this was where she would find it. The empty bottle of toilet water was wrapped in an undergarment of crumpled silk, with slightly yellowed lace. For several moments, Perl felt helpless. She thought that Zsuzsa had won, that there was no point in fighting. Then she put her discovery back exactly as it had been. Without any conscious thought on her part, a decision had already taken shape in her mind.

The next day she went to visit Doctor Averbuch. She confessed to several abortions and the occasional bout of venereal disease, then asked for his advice and the kind of lay absolution for which people used to turn to the medical profession. In the nights that followed, she sought out a surprised and reluctant Sami. One month later she knew she was pregnant. English and North American troops had landed in France and were heading for Paris: Perl wanted to believe her child would be born into a world where Jews no longer felt afraid.

5

ON MAY 18, 1945, AT THE AGE OF TWO MONTHS, MAXI Warschauer made his debut on the stage of the Soleil Theatre in Buenos Aires. He waved a tiny British flag in his mother Perl's arms, while she sang a rough approximation of "Tipperary" in Yiddish.

This *Victory Revue (Siegesrevue)* was not an impromptu affair. Despite the threats from nationalist groups (closely watched by the police ever since the liberation of Paris had made it obvious what the outcome of the war would be, even for those who least desired it in the de facto Argentine government) and weeks before Berlin had finally fallen, Sami Warschauer had started putting together a series of songs and sketches for the regular theatre company to display its talents. He was also hoping that, given the situation in Europe, they could attract a wider public than the faithful families from Abasto, Almagro and Villa Crespo, the neighbourhoods where the poorest members of the Jewish community were concentrated: those whose tastes and aspirations were reflected in the company's shows.

It was a difficult ambition to fulfil at a time when the cinema screens of Buenos Aires were showing films such as *Hitler's Gang*, *Confessions of a Nazi Spy*, *Hitler's Children* and *Days of Glory*. Some of these films were new, others were being given a second screening, after several of them had acquired the unmerited prestige of being banned as Argentina's neutrality veered from side to side. (Prominent among these was the Argentine-made *The End of the Night*, which parachuted the popular singer Libertad Lamarque into occupied France and made her a heroine of the Resistance.) The publicity battle between the big department stores relied heavily on one word: "Victory!" In the Harrods' advert it crowned a flaming torch, and was accompanied by the slogan "Le jour de gloire est arrivé" in French, and "Libertad, libertad, libertad" in Spanish. Gath & Chaves meanwhile used it under a Winged Victory of Samothrace, bust and thighs modestly veiled. From Tunuyán cider to Arizu champagne, all kinds of sparkling beverages also claimed to be the drink with which to toast victory. Sami Warschauer quickly understood that the word "victory" had to be in the title of his revue.

Thirty-five years later, Maxi, who could not possibly have remembered that evening, knew off by heart all the stories about it that had been repeated during his childhood and adolescence by Sami and Perl. He knew, for example, that the show closed with "My heart belongs to you" (*Dein ist mein ganzes Herz*), that indestructible melody from *Das Land des Lächelns*, an operetta known in Argentina as *The Land of Smiles*. In that hopeful month of May in 1945, neither Sami, who sang the words in Yiddish with only slight modifications from the original German, nor the other members of the company, who sang the last verse in chorus in a memorable finale, were aware of something that Maxi himself only discovered years later when he was living in France: the famous composer of the tune had visited Paris only two years before the Buenos Aires show to celebrate the 1001st performance of what was his greatest success after *The Merry Widow*. While he was there, that same Franz Lehár had conducted a concert in the Théâtre du Chaillot with musicians from the three branches of the German armed forces, all of them in dress uniforms as they played beneath a huge swastika adorning the stage. Did the aged composer recall at any point during that evening those far-off days when he had begun to follow in the footsteps of his father, a band-leader in the Austro-Hungarian army?

(Ignorance can provide a fortunate refuge. Sami Warschauer's enthusiastic company, enriched by his and Perl's baby, could not have realised either on that heady evening in May 1945 that one of the original songwriters of *The Land of Smiles*, Fritz Löhner, had been gassed in Auschwitz only a few weeks earlier. Another of the writers, Viktor Hirschfeld, had some time earlier adopted the pseudonym of Victor Léon, although in his case this was more out of an innocent love of France than any desire to be cautious.)

Thirty-five years later, Maxi Warschauer wished he could have the benefit of a similar sliver of ignorance whenever he appeared on a makeshift stage in Paris to a very mixed audience. This was in a run-down café-concert in the Les Halles area, whose name conjured up images of Buenos Aires in a vague way that was perhaps aimed at a public anxious for something slightly less exotic than what was offered by the Brazilian restaurants which seemed to be springing up all over the place, perhaps at those political exiles who looked back with nostalgia to a non-existent militancy. Every night in this cramped dugout, Maxi came onto a badly lit platform to present a group, or occasionally a singer, most of them musicians clinging to the illusion that their appearance in the "City of Light" would guarantee them fame on the distant shores of the River Plate.

His presentation consisted of a genre that had already disappeared: the kind of "commentary" spoken by out-of-work actors during the heyday of radio. The intention in those days had been to put the listener in the mood for whatever composition was about to follow; the people who contracted Maxi saw it as a way of honouring a tradition that could lend authenticity to the club. The dark suit, given a more presentable look by the discreet stage lighting rather than by frequent visits to a dry-cleaner, the yellowing white silk scarf, hair cream that was now coming to be known as gel and which again only thanks to the miracle of theatre could be taken for old-fashioned brilliantine, combined to give Maxi Warschauer that real Buenos Aires "look". To round it all off, he had adopted the stage name of Andrés Machado.

On more than one occasion, following the disappointingly early departure of the last paying customer, Maxi decided to stay on with the musicians and launch into an improvised duet of "Drunk One Last Time". Although it may well have been that "drawing a curtain on the heart" was a good description of the daily disappointment he felt during this miserable after hours, an instinct for survival always took him back to his room in the Hôtel des Deux Impasses in the eleventh *arrondissement*, to the mended sheets, the lumpy mattress and complaining bedsprings. He would fall asleep almost at once, but not before he had dedicated a brief moment to thoughts of his wife, from whom he might be separated but to whom he was irredeemably faithful.

"That *goy* girl is going to be a headache for you." That was one of the last remarks he heard from his mother, a few weeks before she died and only a few hours before she mentally abandoned her identity as Perl Rust and took refuge in being Perla Ritz, a theatre name that had always appeared ridiculous to Maxi, although he had to admit it had once been more successful for her than Andrés Machado was turning out to be for him. The "*goy*" had a name: Graciela Jijena. A few years earlier she had answered the call of an unexpected vocation as a political militant, and then had left Argentina almost immediately for exile in Spain. This period in her life had distanced her for ever from Maxi, whose scepticism was unacceptable to the heralds of the era of the New Man.

Maxi knew she was in Barcelona, working as an editorial assistant in a slim magazine whose title (*Evita Capitana*) was enough to signal how tenuous its links were with any notion of reality. A mutual friend had sent him some copies, full of photographs of no-longer young men, bearded or smooth-shaven, dressed up in fantasy uniforms and giving military salutes to a portrait of the Deceased while offering sickly smiles to the camera. The same friend told him that Graciela also cleaned the modest editorial office, prepared morning coffee for the "comrades", and sewed on the occasional button for them. Maxi also wondered without too much bitterness whether she also slept with some of them, or whether their revolutionary discipline forbade this. In some strange way, which he refused to analyse because he dimly suspected that he might be embarrassed by the conclusions, he found himself falling asleep almost every night believing in this prohibition.

For a few nostalgic Latin Americans, at the end of the seventies in Paris there still existed the remains of a *vie de bohème* that was soon to succumb to the new rigours and frail hopes arising at the end of the twentieth century. In those days before the fall of the Berlin Wall and the subsequent arrival of accordionists from Transylvania and gypsies from the Crimea, it was still possible for your ears to be assaulted in the métro by the music of Andean flutes, charangos and drums produced by rough-looking South Americans in their synthetic alpaca ponchos, or to be handed a leaflet in a café on the Boulevard Saint-Michel by a fortune-teller with a name from the most traditional Buenos Aires aristocracy, who would read your palm in her hotel room; or to see at a neighbouring table an *analyste sauvage* born in Chivilcoy, who every afternoon would listen in non-judgemental silence to the secrets of the bored and desperate.

During this state of artificially prolonged adolescence, Maxi learnt from a postcard that the "*goy*" had gone to make the revolution in Nicaragua. That was the last sign of life he had from her until around 1995, when he discovered her in a photograph in the *Figaro Magazine*, interpreting for an Argentine economy minister on a European tour. He recognised her at once, not so much aged as stretched by whatever surgery was the fashionable belief at the time. He was not taken aback by this, realising that time must have wrought even more changes in himself, by now the director of the French offshoot of a German record company.

The dubious charms of the bohemian life in Paris promised him by films and novels from another time had slowly faded. In his daily life they were reduced to an unappealing sham; at the same time Maxi increasingly felt the need for a certain stability, a planned existence, everything he had not known in his childhood. Slowly and unconsciously, he became immersed in a European greyness, and it was only in nightmares that he was visited by the painted, moth-eaten backdrops that for several generations of undemanding audiences had suggested the outlines of operetta palaces. In his nightmares, too, he saw again the multi-coloured rayon of Perl's skirt with its torn sequins, and Sami's iridescent dinner jacket: everything that had lulled him to sleep in his early years, like a wicked fairy-tale.

He had even tried to get rid of all traces of Andrés Machado. For some time now he had been married to a Frenchwoman who despite their years together still saw him in a mysterious, exotic light; her faithfulness to an illusion gratified him. He had a daughter with his French wife, and the girl could not speak a word of Spanish. Maxi was delighted to think that in addition to his Yiddish he had managed to destroy a second link with his roots. When travelling for professional reasons, he preferred to speak English: he was afraid that if he spoke German, of which he had a better knowledge, the shadow of Yiddish would be bound to take over, catapulting him back once more to that childhood nightmare of crowded dressing-rooms, theatre stages and a school where they had tried to impose a religion that brooked no argument.

Every month, Maxi sent a substantial money order to his father, but only wrote him a card at the end of each Christian year. After the death of Perl, Sami lived alone in the Calle Malabia apartment where he had arrived as a temporary measure forty-five years earlier. The women who brought a semblance of life to his widower's existence could never put up with him for more than a couple of months, and when arthritis struck he had to accept the move to an old people's home in Avellaneda. Maxi used to imagine him talking in Yiddish and retelling all the stories about the Soleil theatre, or perhaps singing along to a crackly, scratched, but still audible seventy-eight record of one of Benzion Witler and Shrifele Lerer's hits to a public of docile old folk. With any luck they were deaf, almost certainly they would all be less talkative than his father. Sami had forgotten about his days as a bandoneon player and the "houses of ill-repute"; all he remembered was his second life, the one Perl had made for him.

6

ONE EVENING IN JANUARY 2000, ON THE ROAD BETWEEN
Paris and Roissy, Maxi could feel his car skidding and stop-
ping at the same time, out of control. He struggled to bring
it to a halt at the side of the motorway. In earlier times, he
thought, or at least in the cinema of earlier times, a long
whistle would have warned him of a puncture. Then he
corrected himself: even if modern technology had not made
that noise a thing of the past, the rain beating down on the
car would have made it inaudible. The rain was not only
pouring down on the car roof and bonnet; it was coursing
down the windows in slow, endless, almost caressing
streams that blotted out the dark landscape in this winter
dusk. It was only a short while before the last feeble light
of day gave way to darkness.

There was no sign of the rain easing up. Stuck on the
A4 several hundred metres from the *périphérique*, he would
have to seek professional help. He should have called the
company he was insured with (every time he had to renew
the policy it seemed like a waste of money, so this was the

first time he felt the money was justified), but his mobile had no coverage. Perhaps he ought to wait for the rain to slacken . . . As other cars roared past him in the darkness, he could make out two tall steel and glass towers which usually told him he was arriving in Paris. Shrouded in the mist, they now seemed to him hopelessly distant, as if they belonged to an urban territory his accident was excluding him from.

In fact, he was quite relieved. He was going to miss his flight: he was going to have to postpone, or perhaps with a bit of luck even cancel, a journey that had created a vague but insistent fear in him. Three months earlier his company had successfully launched a collection called "The Incunables of Tango". After the good reception of the first restorations of originals that were rare but not impossible to find, the company's plans became more ambitious. Someone remembered Maxi's Argentine origins, so inevitably he was the one chosen to go and negotiate with collectors who were less greedy than unpredictable, often simply jealous or even overtly hostile to the idea of sharing their treasure troves with an unknown public, especially as they themselves did not listen to their precious possessions out of fear of breaking or scratching a fragile disc.

Taking their cue from Julio Nudler and his book *Jewish Tango*, of which they all possessed heavily underscored copies, the company's experts had decided that next on their list should be the few records that Rosita Montemar had made. Maxi was enlisted to go and bargain with a particularly difficult collector. He had been sent photocopies of the pages where Nudler talks of the singer. From them he learnt that Raquel ("Ruchele") Spruk, from the Buenos Aires neighbourhood of Villa Crespo, had begun her career as a child actress. She spoke Spanish and such an awful Yiddish that her struggle to pronounce it became the main attraction of all the sketches she performed in at the Soleil. Soon afterwards, she launched into a career as a tango singer with the stage name of Rosita Montemar. The height of this came in 1931, when she won second prize behind the obvious winner, Libertad Lamarque, in a festival organised by *Caras y Caretas* at the Colón Theatre. Rosita was convinced her voice did not sound as good on records, and by the end of the thirties she had decided not only to stop recording, but to abandon her artistic career altogether, after she married the son of an Italian industrialist who, nevertheless, was a member of the Jockey Club and who insisted she forget both her artistic past and her family origins.

Maxi could not help feeling a certain respect and fellow feeling for her. He had never seen her photograph or heard her voice, but admired the way she had undertaken such a dramatic and definitive change of course. Inside the car, he stretched his legs and breathed a sigh of relief. He was protected from the rain still pouring down outside, and he decided to postpone another attempt to communicate with the emergency service, which he was sure would be pointless. An anecdote related by Nudler gradually took over his thoughts. He pictured a chauffeur-driven limousine parked a few metres from the corner of Calle Pasteur and Avenida Corrientes in Buenos Aires late one afternoon. He saw a lady get out of the car, the collar of her fur coat turned up and her hat veil down over her eyes. She walked to the corner store: sawdust on the floor, open barrels of pickled herring. She was responding to an atavistic need that the head chef of the apartment suite in Palermo Chico could not satisfy. Standing at the counter, she devoured pastrami and *gefilte fisch*, or even a portion of goose gizzard filled with *kasha*. Finally, sated and guilty, she returned to her car. The chauffeur was immediately on hand to tactfully open the door and take her back to the new life she had chosen to follow . . .

No, the reason that Maxi was so afraid of this journey from which a chance accident appeared to have freed him was not the bargaining with the collector, which he guessed would be difficult, but which he thought he could cope with. It was the idea of going back to Buenos Aires after a gap of twenty-seven years that made him grateful for the puncture that had left him stranded on a motorway and allowed him to postpone or even abandon the decision awaiting him in the city he was born and grew up in. Should he visit Sami or not tell him he was there? Should he become for a few days nothing more than one ghost among the many he would inevitably run into, or face up to the unknown old man who had once been his unbearable father? If he did, he would undoubtedly have to resume an identity he had spent years trying to obliterate, to cover with a succession of other identities he could discard at will. He could not see any way out. If he closed his eyes, behind the deceiving protection of his eyelids flickered the moving shadows of a private cinema projector, either the confrontation he feared so much or the endless echoes of his guilt.

Minutes or an hour later (he had lost all sense of time in the darkness) he accepted without surprise the image of a woman walking along the hard shoulder of the motorway in the rain. She might have been young, and was wearing a plastic raincoat and carrying a transparent umbrella. She was looking at him and appeared to be heading for his car. When she came alongside and pressed her face to the rain-swept window, he saw she was very young indeed.

Almost as a reflex, he opened the car door. She got in without saying a word, and started to take off her boots. Her feet were so small they looked to him like a child's. He glanced at her again, or perhaps looked at her properly for the first time. Suddenly, he was afraid. How old could she be? Fourteen, fifteen at most? She looked back at him without smiling, and put a confident hand on his trouser front. He allowed her to undo the zip and pull out his flaccid penis, which little by little seemed to become more enthusiastic, although it did not harden.

"How much?"

He asked the question in order to interrupt what he surmised was a routine, as if he might feel more secure within the limits of a transaction. She murmured something which he had difficulty in interpreting as "thirty euros". Where was her accent from? Was she Romanian? Albanian? Curiosity increased his desire, and he soon felt a proper erection. As she moved in a regular rhythm over his flies, he stroked her dyed, unexpectedly clean hair, and suddenly thought this girl must have a pimp waiting for her in some *boulevard de ceinture*, and that she had probably arrived in France in a refrigerated truck or container.

These images of contemporary wretchedness and slavery excited him still further. Almost without realising it, he forgot all prudence and fear and for the first time in a long while ejaculated into a mouth, the girl's mouth. The sound of the car door opening as she spat outside brought him back to a reality he could still scarcely credit.

"How old are you?"

She pretended not to understand, then laughed and raised fingers on her hands until she got to thirteen.

"I don't believe you."

She laughed again as he put her boots back on, stuffing the fifty euros he had thrust at her into the bottom of each of them. Then he heard her say, in a rough-and-ready German with a foreign accent he was not able to place:

"Every day from five to eight between the A4 and the *périphérique*."

Suddenly she was no longer there. She had gone before he had seen her leave, before her last words had raised fresh questions in his mind. Did she speak German, like so many people from the East, as a first step towards the conquest of the other, richer half of Europe? How old was she really? She couldn't have been more than sixteen in any case . . .

As he sat all alone, mobile phone in hand, he remembered that was how old his daughter Cécile was. She did not dye her hair, but the summer holiday sun, one year in the Sahara, another in the Yemen, had lightened it from its original auburn. And even though he found it hard to accept, he could not help thinking that during those expeditions his daughter slept with her travelling companions. She laughed at him, but with a hint of tenderness, in the way that adolescents do with older people they are fond of. *Tu es l'homme de ma vie, le seul*, she would say with a laugh, then give him a long kiss, her cool lips resting on his already wrinkling skin, and hugging him until beneath her thin summer top he could feel the growing firmness of her breasts. Then, too, he thought he could detect on her body pressed against him a dark, distant perfume, and he became afraid, because he knew what that perfume aroused in him, even today.

He found himself unable to check a gesture that by now was mechanical rather than willed: he again dialled the emergency number on his mobile. He was told they would be there in half an hour at most. He realised he had set in motion the chain of tiny gestures and actions that made up his daily life, that took him back to it, that would save him from all harm.

The pouring rain was not only bouncing off the car body. It curled in thick, lazy waves down the windows so that all he could make out were rapid trails of coloured lights, even though the steady drumming noise prevented him from hearing the fleeting bursts of the other vehicles' engines. He could have stayed until the next morning in the middle of this no-man's-land, protected by the metal shell of the car and its heating. How long had it been since he had allowed himself a pause in his journey, in any of the innumerable insignificant journeys he undertook every day? There was no great need to return to his apartment. No one was waiting for him: his wife was in Biarritz visiting her parents; his daughter was heaven knows where. The bachelor life he had been so keen to recover suddenly seemed to him negligible compared to this suspension of time and place, and of the identity he had so laboriously constructed: a limbo of which he had been granted a fleeting glimpse, like water slipping through his fingers, gone in an instant.

At that moment he could not have imagined he would try to rediscover this limbo, and start to return more and more frequently to the A4 and the *périphérique* during the hours the girl had said she would be there. To no avail. Several months later, he thought he saw her again in a *tabac* near Porte de Bagnolet. He caught sight of her from the car, then turned to drive past the lit-up window a second time, then found somewhere to park. From outside on the pavement, he tried to pick out her face: she was standing at the bar, gazing disconsolately into an empty coffee cup.

I am sure that when he went in, and even before going up to her, he was surprised to hear a song in the background that he had not heard for years. On a radio, through all the noise from the till and the shouts of the truck-drivers, he could hear the melancholy strains of a bandoneon and an aged voice soaked in alcohol. The voice was struggling to articulate words that Maxi heard without realising they were a warning: they were foretelling the radical change his life was about to undergo. It is normal he did not understand this, because these discreet signs that destiny sends us can only be read with the passage of time, when it is already too late for them to act as a proper warning.

"Enough of nights full of oblivion
enough of alcohol with no hope,
let what you once were bleed to death
in that faithless yesterday . . ."

PART THREE

I

November 4, 1949

AT ELEVEN IN THE MORNING, ONLY A FEW STEPS FROM THE
corner of Corrientes and Pueyrredón, the Café León was almost in dark-
ness: the light from outside was only dimly reflected in its dilapidated mir-
rors. As I moved away from the door, the deafening traffic noise and
impatient passers-by, it seemed to me the clientèle changed as well. Close
to the windows sat those still interested in all the movement in the streets
outside. I could tell from their conversations they were caught up in small
matters of business or daily intrigues which allowed them to survive and
perhaps even prosper, like all the characters in the neighbourhood. Deeper
inside the silent depths of the room, however, I found figures that seemed
to be almost part of the décor, people who seemed not to have arrived that
morning but could have been sitting for an eternity at their tables with
their coffees or tiny glasses of slivovitz. They sat in silence: some of them
had copies of Di Presse open in front of them (from what date?) but it
was hard to tell if they were actually reading anything.

I had no difficulty recognising Theo Auer. Everything about him spoke of a professional matchmaker: the black suit that was too heavy for the season and too formal for this time of day, the white shirt with cuffs and collar bearing traces of years of regular washing and ironing, even the stiff silk tie held by a tie-pin whose pearl had long since lost its shine. All this revealed a wish to appear respectable, a silent effort to inspire confidence. When I came close to him, wafts of York cologne confirmed my intuition.

"I can see a ring on your finger. If you're married, why do you want to consult me?"

Auer had leapt straight in: these words, spoken not so much aggressively as warily, forced the stranger I was into a corner. What an unerring theatrical instinct, I thought before responding.

"I'm not here to see the shatkhes," I replied in the same direct way. "I want to meet the playwright. Theo Auer, the author of The Moldavian Pimp."

The indifference with which the old man greeted my answer seemed to me almost too perfect. I had already decided I was faced with a consummate man of the theatre. I was willing to take as much interest in all his evasive answers and lies as in any possible revelation, which I was beginning to think unlikely.

"You were a child when that was put on. I doubt whether your parents took you to see such an unedifying spectacle."

"It was a huge success. At home, my mother and father talked of nothing else for weeks. I begged them to take me to the Excelsior, but you're right, they wouldn't let me go."

"It never reached the Excelsior. It opened in the Ombú on Calle Pasteur — in those days, the street was called Ombú. After that, it was put on in

90

different places. Two hundred performances . . ." He half-closed his eyes before going on: *"An unheard-of hit for Yiddish theatre."*

I screwed up my courage to ask the question I had thought it would take me a long time to broach.

"What about your other plays? I'm sorry to be so ignorant, but I don't know them. I'd love to read them. I've formed a theatre company with my wife and a few friends. I'm trying to get together a repertory of plays, and I thought . . ."

"You're way off the mark, young man," the old man cut in with unexpected firmness. *"In the first place, I don't have any other works. I'm a man with one story to tell: I've told it, and that's that. And secondly, Yiddish theatre is dying out, just like the language. Why on earth do you think that what an old man like me might have written could be of any interest whatsoever to today's public? At best it might interest a few old people of my age, but they hardly ever leave their houses, and even if they did go to the theatre they would hardly be enough to fill two or three performances."*

"You're either too modest or too pessimistic. At this very moment the Joseph Buloff company is filling the house every night with a new play, The Death of a Salesman."

The old man emitted a sound somewhere between a cackle and a clearing of the throat, which might have been an attempt at laughter.

"A New York company will always hit the headlines. Besides, Buloff and that Kadison woman make sparks fly whenever they're on stage together. I saw them back in '32, when they put on Kibbitzer, *and that wasn't in the Soleil but in the Teatro Nuevo, at Corrientes 1500. Just imagine, on the far side of Callao!"*

He paused for his words to have the desired effect.

"Anyway, that play you mentioned . . . I don't wish to speak out of turn, but do you know what it's about? A travelling salesman who finds himself out of work just when he's finished paying the instalments on his car. I don't know if you were around for the golden age of Yiddish theatre. But let me tell you, there was romance, music, emotion, intrigue . . . that was another era."

"I understand your point of view, but I'm not sure I share it. Why not let me form my own opinion? Let me read The Moldavian Pimp *and decide if it interests me for the company. Or not."*

Auer stayed silent for longer than seemed necessary to create a calculated dramatic effect. When he did speak again, his tone had changed. He changed topics, apparently more out of curiosity than suspicion.

"How did you find me?"

"You're not exactly unknown. Although these days not many people remember how successful your play was, you're one of the neighbourhood characters. This is your table in the Café León, and nobody would dare sit here if you weren't present . . . but everyone knows you're here every day from ten o'clock onwards. This is Theo Auer's office, and everyone knows it."

The old man did not seem to flinch at this proof of his fame.

"You're looking for Theo Auer. That was the name I used for my one and only theatre play. Did someone tell you that Teófilo Auerbach, the most respected shatkhes *in our community, had ventured into the theatre world as Theo Auer? Or did you deduce it, with the infallible intuition of youth?"*

I suppressed the irritation that the old man's mocking tone produced in me. His question was the only one for which I had no answer. Lost as to what to say next, I stared at the strands of yellow among his untidy grey hair, his ivory-coloured skin and nicotine-stained fingers. When I spoke again, I think my voice had lost much of its enthusiasm, and my tone was almost confidential.

"I remember when they talked about that play I was not allowed to see, my parents mentioned more than once that it had been written by someone called Teófilo Auerbach."

This was not enough to shake him out of his apparent indifference.

"I imagine they spoke the name with contempt . . ."

"All I can remember is them whispering so I couldn't hear."

"Perhaps your parents belonged to that small group of honest, no, irreproachable members of the community who tried to force the cancellation of the play." The old man's tone had also changed imperceptibly. "You said your name was Warschauer, didn't you . . . ? It means nothing to me. At my age I've started to confuse names or to forget them altogether." He gave another cackle. "Don't look so pityingly at me, you can't imagine what a relief it is. And now you're going to have to excuse me, it's almost noon and a father with children to marry is coming to see me on business."

"One last thing before I leave you in peace. Very often, an author is not the best judge of his work. Let me read The Moldavian Pimp. *I can be insistent, you know."*

"And I can be deaf when I want to be. Have a good day."

* * *

I had seen these handwritten pages in the bottom of the shoe box where Sami Warschauer kept the theatre programmes spanning his career. At first I had not given them a second glance: the handwriting was not immediately deci-pherable, and I was impatient to look at all the pro-grammes, so I put them back at the bottom of the box, where they must have slept for decades. Weeks went by, and on my umpteenth visit to the box, I brought them out again. To my surprise, I immediately saw that they contained something important to me: the meeting between Sami and the author of *The Moldavian Pimp*.

What exactly did they tell me? That at the end of the forties, Sami was hoping to form his own theatre company and was looking for a vehicle; that, as Natalia Auerbach had said, old man Teófilo not only had no wish for *The Moldavian Pimp* to be put on again, but was not happy to have his name associated with the work; that Sami was both an acute observer and more than capable of writing down his obser-vations. This discovery gave me an excuse to call Teófilo's daughter again, so that I could take her a photocopy of this manuscript — after I had removed any unflattering refer-ences to her father's physical appearance.

I had not yet made the call when I received a small but bulky envelope through the mail. It contained a postcard and an audio cassette. The few lines on the card were written in a trembling hand; beneath the scrawl I could make out the signature of Natalia Auerbach. She explained that arthritis made it painful for her to write, so she had pre-ferred to record all she wanted to tell me before she began what she thought would probably be her last journey, to

94

Israel. I felt that this might be something important, so waited with some apprehension until I could find a quiet moment to listen. When I switched the machine on, I was surprised at the firmness of her voice, which contrasted so sharply with her uncertain handwriting.

"LISTEN HERE, YOUNG MAN, I LIKE YOU A LOT AND THAT'S why I want to start by telling you that you're getting into a fine pickle, or into hot water, or whatever expression you young people use these days. One thing was Yiddish theatre, which I personally was never interested in, but which obviously played a role in the life of the Jewish community. Something else entirely was that sinister organisation of procurers which you've heard about but don't seem to understand in the context of the time. It's true that the work my father wrote – and which he lived long enough to regret ever having done so – could be seen as a link between the two, but that link is completely coincidental. It has no deeper significance."

The almost stern tone with which Natalia Auerbach's voice began the recording did not exactly encourage me to listen to the rest. But either out of laziness or a feeling of respect for the fact that she had taken the trouble to record the message, I felt I had to go on.

"I realised you had never heard of the *Ansiedlungsrayon* or the pale of settlement, that strip of land between Eastern Europe and Russia where the tsars authorised the Jews to settle. That was where most of the migration to both North and South America came from. The Jews were allowed to stay in their villages, in the *stetl*, or in designated neighbourhoods in the smaller cities, but never in Moscow or St Petersburg. There were lots of intelligent young boys who could study but were not interested in the holy texts: what was to be done with them? They were forbidden from entering Russian universities, but if their family had the means, they could be sent to Germany – where when the Kaiser was alive they had no problems – or even to Paris. It was not so easy for young Jewish women. A few of the more audacious among them, or ones who did not have to answer to traditional families, discovered a ruse: the yellow pass. In those days, not so different in my view from the days of the Soviet Union, people needed a passport to go from one city to another inside Russia. But prostitutes, Jewish or not, could travel around freely thanks to a yellow pass the police issued them with. All they had to do was report every fortnight for a check on where they lived. That was how quite a few ambitious young Jewish women came to try their fortune in the big cities: by signing up with the police as prostitutes. Yes, you heard correctly."

As if she could detect my astonishment and confusion, Natalia Auerbach's voice paused for a moment. I could hear her drink a glass of water before she began again.

"Try to imagine a specific case. A young girl living in a *stetl*. While she is doing the housework she likes to sing, and she's always being asked to perform at celebrations. Somebody tells her she has a good voice, that she ought to study music. Her parents are horrified at the idea that they have an artistic daughter, but the seed of praise has already been planted in the girl's head, and it flourishes. She uses the excuse of an aunt's birthday party to visit the city of Lodz, and finds a way to visit the conservatoire there. A teacher listens to her, promises her a grant. Her parents become resigned to the idea: she can live with her aunt, who will look after her and keep an eye on her. Once she is installed in Lodz, the girl throws herself enthusiastically into this music which seems to offer her undreamt-of horizons. One evening she goes to see a touring Russian opera company; let's say they are performing *A Life for the Tsar*. The bass singing the role of Ivan Susanin impresses her so much that at the end of the performance she goes to find him and tell him she is studying singing. He may feel flattered by this young, and possibly pretty, woman and invites her to have supper with him in his hotel. He tells her Lodz is not big enough for her, that she should continue her studies in a great city. 'Warsaw?' she asks naively; he laughs and replies, 'Please . . . I mean St Petersburg!' I don't know if anything happens between the two of them that night, but she returns to her aunt's house with a letter of recommendation from the famous bass to the director of the conservatoire in the imperial city, and from that moment on her life is dominated by a single obsession: to go and live there."

The sound of a click told me that Natalia Auerbach had paused her recording. For a few minutes, or a whole day? There was no way of knowing, and it did not matter anyway. When the voice started up again, it was obviously not at the same distance from the microphone, and was possibly in a different spot in her apartment. Her story, however, picked up from exactly where she had left off, as though before starting once more she had listened to the last few phrases she had already recorded.

"We will never know how she got to hear about the existence of those yellow passes. Nor how she discovers a madame willing to sign the necessary certificate for the police to issue her with one. What I do know is that she has to hand over her modest savings to the madame for doing her this favour, and that she leaves her aunt two letters: one for her, and the other for her parents. She must also have felt a mixture of fear and a heady sense of freedom as she spent an endless night in the third-class carriage of the train taking her to the Russian capital. When she arrives, the director of the conservatoire does not question her too closely on where she has come from. He gives her work copying music sheets and recommends a room for her in a boarding-house up on the top floor of a newly built apartment block in the east of the city near a tallow and soap-making factory. The girl is poor, sleeps only a few hours every night, and is happy. The fortnightly visit to the police is quickly over with: there are only a few moments of humiliation, lewd jokes, the occasional pawing to put up with. Afterwards, she strolls along the Nevsky Prospekt and sees glimpses of a life that is very different from hers, but which does not arouse any envy or resentment in her. She needs only look down at the rushing waters of the River Molka in this time of thaw to feel that at the age of twenty she has already lived more than what she could ever have expected two years earlier in the *stetl*. She has no idea that her life is about to take another unexpected turn. She meets a young man who is only slightly older than she is. He talks to her about things she has never heard of before: about Bakunin, Kropotkin, about Zionism and socialism, and how their two utopias could possibly coincide. As always, love appears like a window someone opens for us onto an unknown world. The girl starts to miss classes and to neglect her copying; she stays up late at night working as a volunteer in a clandestine printing press. One day she is arrested, together with other anarchists, but when the police see her yellow pass they laugh: 'No whore could ever want a revolution!' But this time they don't let her go so easily: the chief of police has his way with her, then passes her on to his two assistants. This experience completely destroys any sense of security the young woman has. She goes to look for her boyfriend, and tells him what has happened. He takes her in his arms, kisses her, tells her about Argentina. He says they can emigrate there using fake papers he can get from one of the typesetters at the press."

Another pause, this time with no click. A few seconds later Natalia Auerbach added in a lower, almost shy whisper: "that girl was my mother; the young man, my father". It was only then that I heard the click.

* * *

"In Buenos Aires, despite their libertarian convictions, my parents were married in a synagogue. Then something curious took place. My father had been the one who introduced my mother to social and political thinking, but he gradually lost interest in being an activist. She, meanwhile, perhaps due to the humiliation she had personally suffered because of the yellow pass, began to take an interest in how prostitutes were treated in Argentina. You will have heard that in those days there were two big groups who ran the local market between them: one run by pimps from Marseilles, which brought girls from France, or passed them off as French, because they were the most sought after. Then there were the Jews, who started off as two different organisations which eventually became one: the famous, or rather infamous, Zwi Migdal. The Jewish community was up in arms against them. Following the Tragic Week in 1919, when nationalist groups went out to kill Jews in the streets of

Once and Almagro districts, it was imperative to keep the image of Argentine Jewry spotless: they wanted nothing to do with communists who were attempting to repeat the Russian revolution on the banks of the River Plate, or with procurers. These latter could not of course hope to enjoy the cachet that the former had: it was much easier for the good bourgeois in the community to look down on the sex trade than it was on the fight for social justice in which many of their sons and daughters were engaged, however ill-judged they thought it. My mother was indignant at all the complaints that got nowhere, the struggle against the pimps and their allies in Buenos Aires high society, in the law and the police. She saw too many lawsuits that ended in failure, too many congresses whose final resolutions ended up in the waste-paper baskets of those who could have done something about them. Just look at a few statistics: in 1929 it's estimated that there were about 500 members of Zwi Migdal, who controlled about 2000 brothels and 20,000 women in Argentina. There was a synagogue in the organisation's headquarters, where rabbis who aided and abetted them – who knows if they were real rabbis? – performed marriage ceremonies that had no legal status under Argentine law, but were a way of tying the prostitute to her pimp according to their religion. Perhaps my mother remembered the 1905 *Alphonsenpogrom* in Warsaw. That was a unique event: hundreds of Jewish workers stormed and destroyed the brothels run by a man called Alphonse, whom they hanged from a butcher's hook. They wanted to cleanse the community's honour . . . Well, one fine day, on the excuse of obtaining a religious annulment of her marriage, my mother went to visit the rabbi who had married her . . . This man explained that according to Jewish religious law, the wife could take no initiative whatsoever: the process for obtaining the *get* could only be started by the husband, and if he abandoned his wife or died, she became *agunah*, without any possibility of marrying again. For a long time my mother listened to him with feigned resignation; then at some point in his explanation, she killed him."

This time it was me who stopped the recording. I needed a break. When I went back to listen to the cassette some hours later it was as if I were returning to the documentary sources, to the police report of something I had learnt about only when it had been turned into fiction: the way Teófilo Auerbach publicly took the blame for his wife's crime, the way she was declared insane and sent to a village in Santa Fe province, the way a cover-up was orchestrated so that the activities of the "pimps' synagogue" would never become public knowledge. Auerbach only spent two years in jail. It was the members of the Zwi Migdal themselves who arranged his release as a reward for keeping silent. Natalia Auerbach's voice sounded increasingly tired, and ended with an entreaty:

"All this was so long ago it doesn't matter any more. But I know there are people who have not kept a good opinion of my father. I want you to know the truth: it was a crime of honour, a crime by which my mother hoped to gain revenge on behalf of countless victims. She wanted to destroy symbolically all those who were besmirching the reputation of a community which needed, and will always need, its sons and daughters to live by a far more demanding code of justice than anyone else. In a few days' time, I am going to Israel. That's where I want to end my days as a freethinking, non-religious, socialist feminist, fighting against those racist shits who have usurped power there. I can imagine the way you're smiling. Don't worry, I may be old and sick, but I'm not completely gaga. If one day you read that a crazy old woman has shot Sharon, spare me a thought."

3

NATALIA AUERBACH'S RECORDING, WHICH HAD MOVED me so much as I listened to it, nevertheless left an ambiguous aftertaste, as if I somehow mistrusted the emotion it aroused. I tried to understand this feeling. I listened again to her voice, sometimes breathless, at others full of a retrospective, almost posthumous passion. I tried to get beyond the effect it had created in me. Although it seemed somehow unworthy to mistrust her story, I could not avoid the sensation that I was being treated to a performance. It was as if this old woman, who had put so much distance between herself and her father's only adventure in the theatre, had decided to launch herself in what was at one and the same time a tardy debut and a farewell performance. But what role was she playing? What was the plot of her unannounced play? And above all, what was she hoping to get out of this fiction?

I got a pencil and a piece of paper and started jotting down the stories and characters, her comments and possible motives, and creating a different, possibly more real structure. An alternative interpretation began to emerge. I soon realised that her voice, which so often pronounced the name of her father, never mentioned that of her mother: "that girl was my mother . . ." and other similar phrases alluded to her without directly mentioning her. I also thought I could detect cinematic echoes in the description of how her parents met, which seemed so romantic in such a sordid context. Above all, I still found it incomprehensible that such a light, frivolous musical comedy as *The Moldavian Pimp* could be dismissed as a "youthful error" by a woman of such forthright convictions.

What sense did it make for someone to lie when they felt they were on the verge of leaving this life, and wanted to confide a family secret to a near-stranger? As I was asking myself the question, I suddenly realised the obvious answer: it was the last possible moment to try to remedy the past, to build a statue to her absent parents that went beyond mere documental truth. Could it be that the so-called family secret was nothing of the sort, but instead a myth invented to outlast her life, even if only for the few more years my own fragile existence could give it? Especially if the person transmitting that myth was given all the more authority because he had no blood ties to the character whose past was being honoured or more simply whitewashed, to whom a verbal monument was being erected. Yes, all at once I could sense my remaining doubts evaporating: Natalia Auerbach's confession *in extremis* was a fiction whose aim was to cover up the real family secret.

What was behind the spontaneous words that she let slip on my first visit to her, when she said that she wished Bertha Pappenheim had been her mother? What if her real mother, that young girl whose name I do not know, who studied in St Petersburg thanks to the humiliating protection offered her by a yellow pass and who had to suffer all those police controls . . . what if she had been a real rather than an imaginary prostitute? And what if that generous, idealistic, poetic young man who offered to take this unfortunate girl to Argentina had in fact been a pimp? To what extent had Natalia's father, using the transparent pseudonym of Theo Auer, given an idealised portrait of himself in that "Moldavian pimp", a man who ends up falling in love with his charge, to the extent that he takes the blame for her crime, and whose other prostitute victims queue up outside the prison to demonstrate their loyalty?

In my notebook, the lines and arrows linking dates and the names of all these different characters, as well as the cities they had lived in, offered me other interpretations. By showing this assumption of someone's else guilt in his musical comedy, could Theo Auer have been leaving a hidden key to his wishes? Could his daughter Natalia be the one to bring these to fruition? Did the crime of honour Natalia was using to pay homage to the memory of her parents really have such noble motives as she insisted?

Again, I was asking myself the possible reasons for this assuming of someone else's guilt, when the answer suddenly struck me: as a victim, a prostitute does not need a bold gesture to arouse sympathy; a pimp, however, is a killer, but a gesture such as this might redeem him.

I remembered that in the Hebrew Society I had spoken to a reader who had shown a kindly interest in my research. I found the card he had given me: Doctor Salo Dreizik. He had impressed me with his knowledge of rarely consulted archives: on that occasion, for example, I was surprised to find him looking up the genealogies of immigrants in the Hebre Kedische registers. I took the liberty of calling him. I explained that during my searches I had discovered the existence of a theatre play whose success with the public was as odd as the protests it aroused among the Jewish community. I told him I was curious about the author, Theo Auer, whose name did not appear in the Society of Authors register. Far from being put out by my curiosity, Doctor Dreizik seemed pleased to have the opportunity to show off how complete his files and records were, and the access he had to sources unknown to the general public.

A week later he phoned back to confirm everything I had not told him but already knew: the man's real name was Teófilo Auerbach; towards the end of his life he had been a matchmaker; his lack of interest in the theatre, which he had only ventured into on one occasion – the one I had already uncovered. But he also provided one piece of information that Natalia had left out of her recording: Auerbach's wife had been one Rebeca Durán, a Sephardic Jew originally from Constantinople whom some immigrants recalled having seen as a cabaret singer in Warsaw. The lists of passengers kept by the steamship companies showed that she arrived in Buenos Aires from Danzig on the same boat as Teófilo. They were married in a synagogue that no longer exists, in the 3200 block on Calle Córdoba . . .

This last detail came as a real shock: at the same time as it apparently confirmed my intuition, it also gave me pause for thought. One last scrap of information completed the picture: at some point in the twenties, most probably prior to the launch of the musical comedy I had stumbled across, Rebeca Durán de Auerbach, who suffered from incurable bouts of depression, left her husband and daughter and went to live in Santa Fe province. Her grave is in the town of Granadero Baigorria, formerly known as Paganini.

4

IT WAS NOT JUST PAGANINI THAT HAD UNDERGONE A military name change. The Calle Pichincha, close to the Sunchales railway station which as a child I had heard my grandfather from Rosario whisper about as the centre of low life in his native city, had grown in stature and was now the Calle Teniente General Ricchieri. No one seemed to know if it was named after an officer in General Roca's army who had slaughtered all the Indians who came within reach, or a 1930s police chief who had distinguished himself in the fight against the pimps. Whichever was true, in what for me was still the legendary Calle Pichincha I found the Petit Trianon had become an art gallery and cultural centre, and that Madame Sapho's establishment, once the most famous brothel in Argentina, had declined into a cheap hotel. Its attractions had once been "exclusively French women and their darting-tongued dogs", and several generations had imitated, in a Marseilles accent, the phrase clients heard spoken by the madame on the till when they asked for the services of a Georgette or Yvette: "with doggie or without doggie?"

But I wanted to visit Granadero Baigorria before I wallowed in these scenes of low-life nostalgia. On my way there, I found restaurants and picnic areas on the banks of the River Paraná around the bridge that after decades of planning had finally been built to provide a link with Victoria in Entre Ríos province. The sun was baking hot, but a light breeze blew from the river. I yielded to the temptation of eating a grilled *pacú*, a fish even more difficult to find in Buenos Aires than the *surubí*. It must have been three in the afternoon by the time I reached the cemetery of the town that for me was still called Paganini and was the last hideout of the pimps and their clandestine haunts, driven out of the city of Rosario in 1930 by the morality campaigns. I should have said not one but several cemeteries: they seemed to fill an entire neighbourhood, and to give employment to quite a few flower-sellers and funeral masons.

The so-called Jewish cemetery was behind the Christian one. Communication between the two was by an iron gate, now closed and padlocked. The almost inaccessible main entrance gave onto a dirt track that ran alongside the railway embankment taking trains between Rosario and Sante Fe. It was marked by a double-fronted metal gate topped by a six-pointed star and ornate ironwork. I went back to the main road. My request to visit the apparently abandoned terrain was immediately greeted with great suspicion in the cemetery office: I would need two permits, one from the Jewish community, the other from the town hall. When I adopted what I thought was a convincing air of innocence and said my grandfather was buried there, the only response was a smile: "if he was there, you wouldn't be looking for him . . ." It was obvious the people I was talking to knew exactly which part of the huge cemetery I meant, but it was not until I slipped a twenty-peso note across the table ("sorry to bother you, but it's very important to me, perhaps you can see what you could do") that one of the assistants disappeared in silence to search for a bunch of keys in a drawer.

"Ten minutes, no longer," he warned me as he undid the padlock, "and no photos." He stood by the railing watching me walk down paths choked with high grass. None of the gravestones showed any inscription later than 1950. All the enamel photographs had been disfigured with a sharp implement or simply burnt, perhaps with a blowtorch. To my surprise, all the inscriptions mentioned, in Hebrew and Latin characters, the birthplace of the deceased. I had imagined that, given the profession these people had, and the discreet, not to say secret, location of their burial ground, that they might have preferred to keep this a secret, but evidently this was not the case. Who knows what nostalgic impulse from their childhoods, the first landscapes they had known, a time when they could recall themselves as different from how they had ended up, was awakened in their final moments, or more precisely in the compassion of those who had fulfilled the funeral rites on their behalf? How else to explain the urge to engrave on the headstone that Jana W. was "from Podolia", or Mauricio J. "from Bessarabia"?

I searched rapidly among the names and inscriptions. I was sure I would find the words Rebeca Durán, without the married name Auerbach. I was right, and as though to confirm what Doctor Dreizik had told me, beneath the name I read "from Constantinople". There were so many cuts and slashes on the enamel picture I could not make out her features.

Standing there, I recalled a scene from my childhood I thought I had completely forgotten. I was eight when my maternal grandfather died – the only tenuous link we still had as a completely assimilated family with our Jewish tradition. My father was an Italian Catholic, but he did not object to my mother taking me to Liniers cemetery for the funeral. Her grief and filial piety did not completely over-whelm a mother's frugality: realising that a piece of my jacket would be cut off as part of the ritual and thrown into the open grave, she dressed me in my oldest clothes, which for months had been too small for me, and which I no longer wore.

During that first visit of mine to Liniers, I took advan-tage of the fact that my relatives were either praying, or keeping a respectful silence while the dead man's body was being ritually washed, to slip away from an aunt and go to see whether a row of tombstones lined up against the back wall of the cemetery also had graves and names, numbers and photographs like the rest. I trod carefully through weeds still sodden from a recent shower, and leaned on the stones I wanted to decipher, peering down and looking all round me. I soon saw that they were no different from the headstones arranged along the paved paths of the cemetery for everyone to see: they showed the faces of men and women in photographs that as a young boy I could not have guessed had been copied, enlarged, and often coloured by hand. I could, however, see that these people, too, all had the looks of studied seriousness, of steadfast decorum, which their relatives considered appropriate to remember them by.

"You're getting your new shoes soaked," were the words I heard as I was dragged back with a sharp tug to the funeral ceremony. That day I did not have the chance to ask who those tombs with their headstones turned away from us belonged to, and when, a long time later, I did try, the only response I got was "people who are not worth remembering". I know now that at a later date than when those poor unfortunates were buried, the Jewish community split definitively from their outcasts: instead of gravestones turned to the wall, they insisted on separate, isolated, forgotten burial grounds.

5

I DON'T KNOW ANY CITY THAT IS NOT AT THE SAME TIME several contradictory, divided cities, where if you change neighbourhoods you travel to a different country, where you no longer see the faces you meet every day but meet other people you had forgotten and thought were dead.

Not long ago in Buenos Aires, at 2300 on Avenida Rivadavia, I discovered a plaque on the wall of a branch of the Banco de Galicia. It said that on this spot had once stood the Marconi Theatre, previously called the Doria. I knew the legend: until midway through the last century, when its opera seasons finally closed, the Marconi had been a refuge for ageing singers, world-weary artistes not yet resigned to retirement. This was where they ended their careers, contemptuous of the enthusiastic amateurs who played the other roles in the productions, determined to throw themselves for perhaps one last time into *I Pagliacci* or *Cavalleria rusticana* for a sparse public of nostalgic old folk who had once been immigrants.

Far from the Colón Theatre and its demanding, worldly

audience, the Marconi faithful wanted arias they knew by heart and endowed with the recollection or the imagined memory of more prestigious renditions. But long before this final decline, the theatre stage had seen the likes of Pablo Podestá perform, and it was here in 1923 that Carlos di Sarli, "the gentleman of tango" had first appeared when he arrived in the capital from Bahía Blanca to accompany his uncle, the lyrical singer Tito Russomano, on the piano. It was here, too, during the 1926 carnival dances, that Juan de Dios Filiberto had given the first performance of his immortal tango "Caminito".

(All this took place decades before I was born, and these are only memories gleaned from books. The same idle curiosity had prompted me to pursue the history of a forgotten musical comedy written in Yiddish, and this had led me willy-nilly to another story, that of the Zwi Migdal and its web of shame and romance. I don't think I am nostalgic for things I never knew; I am simply attracted by the idea of illuminating them with the uncertain spotlight of fiction. I do, though, admit to an impulse that I can only describe as literary, but which shyness or mistrust has prevented me from putting into writing. Instead, I find myself in this restless state of always passing by, without ever becoming a *flâneur*. I also concede that my studies have been mere pretexts to enable me to question silent photos, faces which cannot see me, old papers, and to project on them a life that no longer exists, a life that seems to me less anodyne than our miserable present. I am not interested in any self-examination to discover the reasons for this way of being, although I doubtless conceal them from myself: I'll happily leave that to any of the countless fellow-countrymen of mine addicted to psychoanalysis.)

There is no plaque commemorating the spot where the Soleil or the Excelsior stood. The building where the Ombú Theatre had been became a Jewish association, which in 1995 was blown up thanks to an obscure plot hatched by Iranian, Syrian and Argentine agents. And of course there are no plaques recalling the shame of the houses "of ill-repute", whose addresses now are only to be found in the police archives or in the less inaccessible crime reports of *Crítica* and *La Razón*. On many nights as I stroll aimlessly along Balvanera and San Cristóbal, I can imagine their ghostly presence behind or underneath the sad apartment blocks. A short while ago, when I visited some friends in an apartment on Junín and Lavalle designed by a famous architect of the 1920s, the odd arrangement of the corridors, the way the different doors communicated with each other, and above all the unusual size of the bathrooms, all led me to suspect it had once had a very different function, now forgotten.

On the evening of the day when I went to the cemetery in Granadero Baigorria I was walking around the old part of Sunchales, reluctant to return to my hotel in the centre of

Rosario. I stopped to drink a grappa in the Wheelwright on the corner of Calle Brown and the street I'll always think of Pichincha, when I thought I saw a light in the Petit Trianon. Looking in through the balcony, I noticed a group of people listening to a lecturer. He was holding a video-cassette and standing next to a television; I remembered that the house had been turned into a cultural centre and art gallery, and so I made up my mind and went in.

I arrived in time to hear the end of his introduction: he was showing a film about elderly French actors exiled in Argentina during the Second World War or in the years immediately after. In spite of the enthusiasm with which he was presenting the showing, I soon lost interest and asked the woman who was director of the centre if I could look round the house. She accepted with that spontaneous kindness that is so common outside Buenos Aires, and explained that the art gallery was in what had once been the "reception rooms", where the men talked politics, played cards, and chose the girls they would then take to the bedrooms.

Those bedrooms still exist. They have been turned into a boarding-house whose narrow street door used to be the "tradesman's entrance" of the old brothel. The director explained that most of the rooms were taken by the "new poor", middle-class people ruined by all the risky adventures that the economists running Argentina had embarked on. She led me down a dark passage to a big yard with rooms on every side. These rooms had no doors, and were protected simply by curtains. The warm, starry night had brought the lodgers out in friendly groups. Many of them were sitting talking or passing round the *maté* gourd, others were listening to their transistors on earphones, while children scampered in and out, laughing and ignored by the adults. In one corner, a group of women were watching another episode of a soap about models and drug-traffickers on a television set. Nobody seemed bothered by my intrusion.

I did not stay long in this oasis of other people's calm. I preferred to say good-bye to my friendly hostess in the street, to avoid disturbing the film audience in the gallery. As a souvenir, she gave me a "token": the flimsy metal coin a client would purchase in order for him to take his turn with one of the girls. At the end of each day the girls had to return them to the madame, who counted them to keep a check on how busy they had been.

"As you can imagine, when work began on the gallery there was no trace of what the place had once been, fifty years earlier. But in the kitchen in what had been a pot for quince jam, I found hundreds of these 'tokens'. They were still in good condition, with no rust on them. Later, I heard that one of the earliest tangos, from the 1910s, was called 'Give me the Token'. You can imagine what that means. I've been told there were lots of tangos that were only played in brothels, with titles that were meant to have

a double meaning but in fact only had one. Forgive me for
not telling you them. The least offensive is by Arolas: 'Hot
Potatoes' . . ."

6

BACK IN BUENOS AIRES, I DROPPED MY NOTEBOOK INTO the same shoe-box where Sami Warschauer had kept his theatre programmes, souvenirs of a life that must have slowly faded from his failing memory. A respectful, perhaps superstitious attachment to anything that might have survived those they belonged to prevented me giving them a new if temporary home in the rubbish bin; but I am sure they had already begun to be erased from my own thoughts too.

The fact is that almost without taking a conscious decision, I had given up my research. I was no longer interested in whether Rebeca Durán, whose real name nobody would ever know, had killed the fake rabbi, or if her husband had found her refuge in that town in Santa Fe province that would later become a home to pimps and crooks. I did not want to know if Auerbach had tried to exorcise his shameful previous existence by means of a theatre play, only to live its success as a humiliation, or if the daughter whose uneventful life contrasted with all the dramas that had marked her parents' lives had decided to rewrite that obscure past that would never become a historical event . . . They were too much for me, these lives I had no way of redeeming. I preferred to keep their secret.

I also felt more than ever how impossible it is for us to know anyone else, to discover the meaning of their actions. How could I know if Rebeca Durán's crime had been a conscious act of rebellion against a trade she had been condemned to be part of? If it was her repudiation of all those who were undermining the rites of her religion? Might it not have been an entirely personal act of revenge for the fake marriage that had tied her for ever to a man who was exploiting her? As for Teófilo Auerbach, had he really been protecting her by sending her to Granadero Baigorria? Perhaps he had simply sent her somewhere new to work, a place where his associates continued using her in return for keeping quiet about her crime. And was it true about Rebeca's depression . . . ?

In short, I do not want to use their lives to write a novel. I prefer to respect silence, to prepare for oblivion. The oblivion awaiting us all.

I felt, however, that there was one debt I had incurred during my researches which I ought to repay. I ought to send Maxi Warschauer the pages his father had written about his 1949 meeting with Theo Auer. Although they were not likely to be of any interest to him, they were hand-written, and to me this lent them a dignity that printed matter never has. I thought the son ought to keep this imprint of his father's hand.

The search for Maxi's whereabouts led to fresh surprises. The last money orders Samuel Warschauer received were sent from the head office of Crédit Suisse in Geneva, and that was where the last two of them, which arrived after his death, were returned to. I knew the tradition of Swiss confidentiality meant I could expect no information from them. I asked for help among my few acquaintances in Paris, but Maxi's name rang no bells there. Finally it was an Argentine student (who had a grant from the École d'Hautes Études en Sciences Sociales to study the renewed interest in the *milonguero* style) who, perhaps because she had a similar detective streak in her, promised she would track Maxi down.

A few weeks later I received an email informing me that a Frenchwoman in her seventies, addicted to the summer tango nights on the banks of the Seine, remembered Maxi from the days when he was a compère at a café-concert in Les Halles. Since then she had lost contact with him, but she thought friends from that time had commented that Maxi had vanished following some ill-defined trouble with the police. Demonstrating admirable tenacity, the student wrote to me again a few weeks later: Maxi was in jail. Here is part of her mail:

"I visited him in La Santé and listened to his story. I found it confused, but fascinating. He held his head high and emphasised every word as he explained that he had tried to rescue a young Kosovar girl from prostitution. He got so involved that in the eyes of the law he was actually mixed up in trafficking young women from the Balkans. At any rate, he had tried to liquidate (I did not know whether he was using the word metaphorically or not) the pimp who was exploiting the girl in question. Whatever happened, thanks to Maxi the girl had been able to start a new life as an usherette in a cinema in Pigalle. She visits Maxi every Sunday (unlike his wife and daughter, who have disappeared from his life) and takes him his favourite cheese-cake, the *vatrushka* that a baker in the Rue des Rosiers makes. I listened carefully to his story: the words he used were those of a man who is no longer young, but who is stubbornly clinging to a romantic image of himself. I don't think I would be wrong in saying that Maxi is somehow pleased with his present situation, however terrible it might seem to anyone else: he's serving a five-year sentence for living off immoral earnings, statutory rape, and complicity in illegal immigration."

A few days later, another mail gave me more results of her investigation. The student, who I suspected was beginning to take a more than anecdotal interest in Maxi, had been searching through back issues of the sensationalist press. She had discovered that this ex-child prodigy of Yiddish revues in Abasto and Villa Crespo, ex-compère of a Les Halles café-concert, ex-abandoned husband of a dilettante guerrillera, ex-executive of a multinational record company, had been involved in the murder of a man called Nathan Lazar, a procurer of dubious origin (he was found to have three passports in his possession, one from the no longer existent Soviet Union, another from the Republic of Moldavia, a third from Romania) who had been stabbed to death in one of the approaches to Porte de Bagnolet. There were no witnesses to the crime; the only evidence was Maxi's confession, about which a police psychiatrist had expressed serious doubts.

To me, the story seemed fanciful, if not completely fabricated: literature in the worst sense of the word. But if there is something I've learnt in the months I spent researching, it is to accept that reality has a tendency to ignore the need for verisimilitude we demand of fiction. I thought, however, that I could detect a strange sense of destiny in this narration: an obscure immigrant, unlucky in love, who had perhaps abused the prestige exile held for well-meaning Europeans, had then tried to construct a new identity for himself that turned out to be just as unfortunate as his previous one. All of a sudden, he had launched himself (even though by now he had supposedly reached the age we call mature) into the only adventure he could find, fascinated by a character from tango romances that chance had sent his way . . .

Maxi cannot have known – he had no possible way of

knowing — that by getting involved in this story he was reconnecting with another one, the one his parents had kept secret. In another continent and another century, and adorned with the false seduction of the novelesque, he was discovering the same misery and the same trade that had marked his own origins . . .

But what right do I have, living vicariously as I do the lives of others gleaned from piles of old papers, to think that I am any more lucid, or that I can understand Maxi? There is no doubt — and now I understand what the student meant — that he is happy in prison, because being in jail gives him the identity, full of risk and violence, he had previously only fantasised about. Suddenly, I was afraid. I could see myself at the still distant and scarcely imaginable age of fifty throwing myself eyes wide open into the dictates of desire, into who knew what adventures where I would be the only one who could see how this was the exorcism for all the notes, libraries and sleepless nights I had lived through. Yes, I felt afraid. But I also felt a spark of curiosity and — do I dare admit it? — a glimmer of hope.

Yes, Maxi must be happy in his cell.

EPILOGUE

ONE STIFLING SUMMER AFTERNOON I PLUCKED UP
courage and headed for Avellaneda. This time I allowed
myself the modest luxury of a taxi, although the driver had
to consult his map and question several pedestrians before
he found the old people's home. Only a few months had
passed since my previous visit, on that brief winter afternoon when, after learning that Sami Warschauer had died,
I stopped for a drink of gin in the corner bar, still carrying
the shoe-box where decades of forgotten theatre history
lay. In spite of my decision not to write about it, not even
about the impossibility of really knowing the story of indi-
viduals whose lives I felt I had been spying on, I was still
finding it hard to get them out of my mind. I thought that
in the Home I might discover some more of Sami's belong-
ings that did not interest them, but which I could send on
to Maxi.

As the taxi approached, it seemed to me the Home was
even quieter than usual. It was not so much that before it
had seemed lively, but now in the harsh summer light I

could see the cracks in its façade, a few broken shutters, dead plants in the cramped garden. It was only when I got closer that I saw a sign hanging between two first-floor windows announcing that it was for sale.

"There were only two old fellows left," the bar owner told me a few minutes later. "A week after your friend died, so did another one. That left only two, and they had no relatives, so they shipped them out to a geriatric place in Quilmes and shut up shop."

The bar itself looked even more run-down and dirtier than I remembered it. The labels on the bottles behind the bar looked more faded still.

"And I've finally made my mind up too. I'm selling up and leaving. It's never too late to start again, so I'm going to Entre Ríos to live with my nephew. His wife's just died."

I wondered if he really thought he would be good company for someone much younger than himself, but preferred to take advantage of his talkative mood to ask about the neighbourhood.

"They've even sold the waste lot opposite. The Jews from the cemetery bought it. They needed more space, and paid a good price for it. The far end of the land is right next to their main cemetery, so all they have to do is knock down the end wall. They did something similar before I came here, with another part of the cemetery that had also been abandoned. I don't know how they managed to find the heirs; the people in the garage reckoned that the original owners had changed their name after they spent some time inside."

The imminence of his departure seemed to have loosened the proprietor's tongue, and he jumped from one topic to another without a pause.

"Would you like a genever? It's on the house. I'm leaving at the end of the month and I don't want to have anything left in the bottles. The people from the salvage yard on the next block are coming on Monday to take the tables: they're real marble, they're worth a fortune nowadays."

It was true: the first time I had come to the bar it felt as though I were stepping back in time, before formica had got everywhere, when I saw marble table-tops that used to be common but are now a luxury, and that looked very odd in this run-down establishment. On top of this recollection I also remembered a passage from a Spanish novel I had read many years earlier. A shiver of fear and intuition ran through me, and then I immediately remembered something else: the way that old man Warschauer had refused to sit at one of these tables, preferring to stand at the bar.

I said nothing, but went over to a marble-topped table. With a strength I did not know I possessed, I lifted the top, which was only resting on the black iron supports. I turned it on its side against the wall. Behind me I heard a startled shout from the proprietor, which soon turned to a gasp of amazement. He left what I had taken to be his permanent place behind the bar and came over to me.

"What . . . what's that?"

The two of us stared in silence at the characters written in Hebrew with a Spanish translation underneath, at the empty oval from which the deceased's photograph had been removed, his name, the dates of his birth and death, and finally where he had originated from: as though even this far away, relegated to an almost clandestine final resting place, he had wanted to have the name of Kishinev engraved on this marble slab that used to be regarded as eternal. I stroked the unpolished stone, and could feel the indentations of the inscription.

I lifted the other table-tops one by one, reading names, dates, and always the name of the place that someone had refused to forget: Lvov, Jassy, Tiraspol, Gdansk, Pécs, Czernowitz, Wrocław, Brody, Warsaw, Castoria, Lemberg, Odessa.

* * *

No sooner had I arrived home than I rang Doctor Dreizik and told him what I had found. He would know what to do next, and I had no wish to get involved with all the different cultural, mutual aid, recreational or social groups, all of them linked by countless, unfathomable intrigues, which could possibly lay claim to some authority over a son of the diaspora who was quite happy to stay that way. The doctor reassured me: the gravestones would be taken to La Tablada as soon as possible, and the bar owner offered compensation to make up for what he would lose by not selling them. While I was thanking him and saying good-bye, I could not help thinking that although the grave-stones would now probably end up in a legitimate burial ground, the remains whose presence they had once sig-nalled would continue, anonymously now, to be scattered in a restless earth that new bodies would soon come to inhabit.

I think I fell asleep at my desk. I woke with a start a few hours later in front of my Mac. But I had not had a night-mare: on the contrary, I dreamt that a very young girl was coming through a field of yellow flowers to meet me. (Could they have been mustard flowers, something I had never seen? Thanks to the unexplained certainty of dreams, I knew the landscape was that of a distant country I had never visited.) The girl had dark hair, with copper tints in it. She had freckled, milky-white skin, and smelt of recently watered grass. She kissed me and whispered words in my ear in a language I did not know, and yet which I somehow understood.

It was the beating of rain against my bedroom window-pane that had woken me. Although it was eleven in the morning, it was dark outside, and a lowering sky was unleashing endless torrents on the streets of Buenos Aires. They were sure to be flooded before long, their drains choked as usual by these extremes of climate that were as predictable as they were ignored. As soon as the pavements had been swept clean, and the authorities had removed the bodies of some poor pedestrian drowned as he crossed Avenida Cabildo or a housewife electrocuted by a snapped electric cable in her doorway on Calle Necochea, it would all be forgotten until the next deluge.

I thought this rain would also wash away much of the abandoned part of the Avellaneda cemetery. The earth had already been disturbed when they dug up the headstones to make room for new burials, decent people whose names could be exhibited without any sense of shame on expensive new tombs, people who would have no idea that in this freshly dug earth they would be rejoining the nameless remains of those whose identities were hidden on the underside of tables in a bar, the enamel photographs of their faces slashed or simply ripped out of the recycled marble.

These respectable dead would no doubt arrive with no knowledge of the happiness an unpunished crime could bring, a crime committed out of pure pride more than seventy years earlier by an anonymous, long-forgotten Jewish woman. By so doing she had hoped to cleanse the honour of a community which was fated not to avoid the common Argentine destiny of corruption and silence, whose representatives would bring fresh shame on themselves when they chose prudent political calculations over the memory of their victims.

I also thought of those humble theatres that had offered

a fleeting, illusory communion to so many lonely people, to the guardians of a language that was on the point of vanishing and in which their children would never speak to them, and that they themselves would never use for communication, if they were still alive and remembered it at all. Theatres so distant from any idea of "low-life" that their promoters would suffer if they knew that today I consider them to have been the purveyors of the same kind of fragile pleasure as the "houses of ill-repute" in the Boca and Once, in San Fernando and the Paseo de Julio, and on Pichincha and Brown in Rosario . . .

Who knows whether in that plot of land concealed behind whitewashed walls in Avellaneda, fertilised by so many condemned bones and consecrated by people who had relegated others from their own religion there, a mingling is not already taking place of the new and old dead with some of those arthritic, varicose-veined chorus girls who crowded the stage of the Excelsior convinced of their irresistible charms, or the decrepit thespians who a visit by Maurice Schwartz had made believe that they too could be Hamlet.

And I wondered how much rain would have to fall, how much earth be dug, how many worms would be needed for something rich and strange to emerge from their decomposing bodies, something untouched by emotions and unsettled scores, something untroubled by any sense of guilt, and not marked by any memorial.

AFTERWORD

EVERY DISPLACEMENT, EVERY ADVANCING ARMY, EVERY immigration and every caravan carries with it a contingent of lesser battalions which, like remoras, attach themselves to the moving convoy and follow it to its port. Pedlars, priests, petty criminals, fiddlers or flute-players, as well as enterprising pimps and their molls, come with the human flow and lend the new society that settles on a strange land a certain familiarity and common grounding that mitigates some of the strangeness, like the effect produced by everyday characters appearing in a foreign play – characters with which the audience can, if not identify, at least establish a conventional relationship. The grandeur or vastness of the movement does not much matter: big or small, every immigration drags with it its corresponding supporting cast.

In 1891, the Argentine government sold to Baron Maurice de Hirsch 1300 square leagues of land in the provinces of La Pampa, Entre Ríos, Santa Fe and Santiago del Estero, for £200 sterling a league, to enable him to set up colonies for the persecuted Jews of Europe, mainly from Russia. Over the next decades, tens of thousands of Jews flocked to Argentina and established themselves in Baron Hirsch's colonies, many of them eventually drifting towards the capital, Buenos Aires. Together with the peasants, artisans and craftsmen came the others, the artists and the prostitutes, and soon the new Zion could boast of one of the best Yiddish theatres in the world and one of the most effective chains of brothels. A notorious organisation, the Zwi Migdal, began a highly efficient system of Jewish white slave traffic that, under the protection of a corrupt Argentine police force, brought into the country, and then exploited, thousands of women.

The chronicle of Argentina's Jewish immigration and its attendant stories is the backdrop of *The Moldavian Pimp*, a chronicle upon which Edgardo Cozarinsky casts a darkly humorous and inquisitive eye. At the centre sprawls the European history of Argentina's Jews, reaching far back into the memory of shtetls and pogroms, of minor heroic gestures and intimate acts of resistance; encroaching it, a gossip of infamous betrayals, enterprises dictated by greed and inglorious personal confessions. Cozarinsky's literary model is neither the documentary novel nor the doleful family memoir, but the Yiddish dramatic tradition of myths and musicals that, translated from the Russian pampas to the Argentine steppes, acquired on the stages of the new country the costumes of local colour and the rhythm of tangos and milongas.

The material upon which Cozarinsky draws his fiction is vast and chaotic, and yet *The Moldavian Pimp* avoids the pomposity and rhetoric of extensive sagas in order better to concentrate on that which is of the essence, the intricate and mysterious core of the story. He gives us nothing superfluous, nothing that might appear as a literary indulgence. In a few pages, the whole history of the Jewish immigration to Argentina is distilled down to a handful of precise events that, if properly understood, must suffice for the discerning reader. In his now classic book on Jorge Luis Borges and film,* Cozarinsky noted Borges's "distrust of the scale demanded by the novel", a bold literary position that "destroys the very possibility of even approaching a genre that, in order to develop character and to proportion its episodes, requires a necessarily unhurried orchestration of specific circumstances and trivial information". This impossibility is exactly what Cozarinsky has here achieved.

Cozarinsky's interest lies not with straight paths and conclusive narratives whose end is visible from the start, but with the crossroads, the double or triple space where different stories meet and, at the same time, seem to part. Incongruous pairings, strange encounters, uneasy coincidences, astonishing repetitions, unexpected revelations and secret links hold Cozarinsky's fiction together, and their exposure results not in an obvious recital of facts, never in the apparently implied turn of events, but in the laying bare of points

* *Borges y el cinematógrafo* (Emecé, Barcelona, 2002)

at which the facts collide and dissolve into one another.

It is as if Cozarinsky were telling detective puzzles from the wrong end of the story, exposing the guilty party first and then taking us forward through a maze of necessary, revelatory clues. Cozarinsky does not mislead the reader. He merely presents the story as a sequence of unveilings in which each new scene, each new character or confession, shows itself not only in its own light but, illuminated by the confessions, characters or scenes that precede it, becomes an independent moment in the story and yet is also an intricate part of the whole. The style reveals the contents. In the final pages of *The Moldavian Pimp*, we realise that History (beyond allegories, History turns out to be this novel's true subject) also proceeds in this strip-tease fashion, each segment suggesting a final truth. Then, just before the end, the lights go out.

ALBERTO MANGUEL